SECRETIVE

SECRETIVE

BOOK TWO IN THE ON THE RUN
INTERNATIONAL MYSTERIES

SARA ROSETT

McGuffin Ink

SECRETIVE

Book Two in the *On The Run International Mysteries* series

Copyright © 2013 by Sara Rosett

Second Paperback Edition: November 2016
First Paperback Edition: February 2013

ISBN: 978-0-9982535-6-5

1

May

Dallas, Texas

He waited until the woman jogged to the end of the block, her red ponytail making her easy to track. When she turned the corner, he checked to make sure there was no one in sight, then left his car and walked briskly up her driveway to her back door. She lived alone, and he had nothing to worry about as he approached the house. No pets. No alarm. He removed a slim case from a pocket and went to work on the deadbolt. Three minutes and he was in.

"So easy," he murmured to himself as he entered the kitchen and saw that the woman had left her laptop on the island. No password protection, either. He made a tsking sound. This wasn't a challenge at all.

With a few strokes, the keylogger was installed. Now, all he had to do was read the reports.

He checked his watch. It had gone so quickly that he had time to take care of her car, too.

Wednesday, First week of November

Dallas, Texas

The ledge was an inch beyond the straining fingertips of Zoe's right hand. She fought the urge to glance down at her feet. That would involve looking at the ground, which was a good twenty feet below and would cause her stomach to do a rollercoaster-like flip. She ignored her quivering calves as she let out a shaky breath and lunged. Her fingertips curled around the ledge, but before she could get a firm grip, her left foot slipped and then she was swinging in midair like the pendulum of a clock, suspended a few feet from the "rock" face in her harness.

A voice floated up from the ground. "Try the yellow toehold for your right foot."

Zoe looked down at Ty, far below, his feet braced and

arms taunt as he held the rope that supported her weight. She shook her head. "No. I'm done. Ready to lower," she called.

"Lowering," Ty replied, letting out a little of the rope. Zoe swung her feet toward the rock wall and gently bounced her way down, then collapsed in a quivering puddle on the padded floor. "Off belay," Zoe said, already feeling the fatigue in her calf muscles, triceps, and forearms. "My toe and finger muscles are sadly out of shape," Zoe said, shaking out her hands, which now sported a few callouses.

"Belay off." Ty unhooked the carabiner from his harness and the rope. A compact man in his late forties, Ty was one of the owners at Rock Sport Center and had literally shown her the ropes last winter when he taught the climbing class she took as an introduction to the sport. "It's been a while since I've seen you."

"Too long," Zoe agreed. Despite her quivering muscles, it had felt good to be out there on that ledge. She'd been playing it safe too long.

"Been doing anything interesting?"

There was no quick or easy way to explain the conundrum that her life had become during the last few months. She settled for saying, "Some travel. Italy."

"Nice. Sure you don't want to go up again?"

"No, I've got a lunch date." Zoe rolled into a sitting position so she could untie the rope and unbuckle the harness. She might be able to finish her copy-editing job before Helen arrived with lunch...if she could manage to type with trembling fingers.

WHEN the knock sounded on her kitchen door two hours later, Zoe paused for a beat to call out, "Door's open," then resumed typing as her friend Helen stepped in the kitchen.

"Give me a sec," Zoe said, squinting at the screen. "Just need to add this bit about the Romantic Road..." Zoe was mid-thought, summing up her most recent copy-editing job for *Smart Travel*'s Germany, Switzerland, and Austria Guidebook. Her fingers were only a little quivery now, but she was glad she didn't have more typing today after she finished this round of edits.

Zoe was vaguely aware that Helen marched across the kitchen and plunked her oversized purse on the island across from Zoe with a firmness that jangled the heavy gold hardware on the designer bag. Zoe finished the sentence with a flourish. "What did you bring—" she broke off as she finally looked up and saw Helen's face.

Helen slapped a narrow folder on the island in the same way that a Regency gentleman might have smacked the cheek of a rival, challenging him to a duel.

Zoe leaned back. "What's wrong?" Helen almost looked as if she wished she could swat Zoe with the paper instead of the island. Under her golden brown bangs, Helen's face flushed, and her lips pressed into a thin determined line. It was so unlike Helen's normally sweet and serene expression that Zoe asked, "Did the cleaners lose your orange Armani jacket again?"

"No. Here." Helen stabbed the folder with her French manicured fingernail.

"What is it?" Zoe asked warily. Helen in this state never lasted long. You just had to wait out the storm—kind of like the tornados that ripped across the Texas plains in the spring. It would all be over in a couple of minutes.

Helen shoved the paper across the island. "That is an intervention."

"Okay," Zoe said slowly.

"Tucker and I are going to Atlantis in the spring."

"That should be an interesting trip, since it's a lost city and all."

"The *resort*. In the Bahamas."

"Oh. I see," Zoe said, despite the fact that she'd never heard of it. Zoe's travel dream destinations centered on other locales, namely Europe. She'd had her fill of tropical islands during her tween years courtesy of her mom's ambition to be a star, which had landed their rather dysfunctional blended family on a "deserted" island for a cable reality show.

"Well, that's great," Zoe said, at a loss for why Helen looked almost furious. "Shouldn't you be happier? I mean, you are talking about a vacation here, right?"

"I'm buying you a ticket. You're going with us. It's my Christmas present to you."

"What?" Zoe opened the folder and took out a glossy brochure. A gigantic pink-hued building on a white beach filled the top of the brochure. On the lower portion, a family immersed in brilliant blue water laughed as they petted the slick head of a dolphin. Off to the side sat a massive water slide designed to look like a Mayan temple.

"It's a little early for Christmas," Zoe said lightly. Helen didn't crack a smile. Unlike Zoe, who had a budget so tight that it might as well be in a straightjacket, Helen had disposable income. A few years ago when Tucker had been fresh out of law school and only a lowly associate, Zoe and Helen had both watched every penny, but Tucker was moving up the ranks at his firm quickly. His growing income combined with Helen's income from her job at the county clerk's office meant that Helen could spend more on a blouse than Zoe did in a month on groceries.

Zoe's glance strayed to the gaping hole in the kitchen ceiling that exposed pipes, two-by-fours, and wiring. Zoe's savings account had covered the water leak and the plumbing repair, but hadn't stretched to fixing the drywall. It had been over a year, and she had nearly enough money to replace the drywall and complete the job. Tropical resort vacations just weren't a possibility on her budget, and she didn't want Helen underwriting a vacation for her either.

Zoe replaced the brochure in the folder with the name of a travel agency on it. "I can't accept a gift like that."

"Why not?" Helen shot back almost before the words were out of Zoe's mouth. "Why the hell not?"

Zoe blinked. Helen hardly ever swore. In fact, the last time Zoe heard Helen swear was when she'd hit her thumb with a hammer while nailing several crates together to create a bookshelf last spring during a Pinterest-inspired decorating bout.

"You're the one who is always going on about your freedom," Helen said, arms braced on the island. "About how you're not a cog in the corporate machine and can do whatever you want. But you don't. You don't do anything except stare at that laptop," she said, her diamond stud earrings flashing as she nodded her head toward Zoe's ancient Dell.

"Whoa. What is going on? Why are you mad at me?"

"I'm not mad at you." Like a pricked balloon, Helen

deflated. "You know me and how much I hate confrontation. I had to psych myself up for this."

Helen walked around the island and plopped down on the barstool next to Zoe. "I know you. If I dropped the vacation idea in the conversation casually and said, 'why don't you come to Atlantis with me?' you'd blow me off. I don't want you to do that. I want you to consider it. *Seriously* consider it." Helen pushed the folder from the travel agency closer to Zoe.

Above the travel agency's name, the wingtip of a jet zoomed upward toward puffy clouds. Several little inset squares marched across the bottom of the folder: coconut palms over a white beach, the Eiffel Tower glowing in the night, umbrellas fluttering over diners at a sidewalk café, the Leaning Tower of Pisa.

For as long as she could remember, Zoe had wanted to travel. As a tween, she hadn't read *TigerBeat* or *Seventeen*. Instead, she'd poured over library copies of *National Geographic* and *Budget Travel*. While Helen had been leaning over the bathroom counter, peering into the mirror, trying to recreate the latest trend in "smoky, sultry eye shadow," Zoe had been lost in the dog-eared, yellowed pages of old romantic-suspense books, transported to England, Crete, Greece, Italy, and even Egypt by the words of Elizabeth Peters, Mary Stewart, and Phyllis Whitney.

Looking back, Zoe wondered if it wasn't exactly travel she yearned for but simply an escape, any escape, from her life. Technically, she had traveled some as a tween, but spending several months on a tropical island with a reality show film crew didn't count as seeing the world, at least not in Zoe's book. That whole experience was as artificial and contrived as a theme park ride. Maybe because of that experience, she'd bundled all her hopes and dreams into 'travel,' hoping to someday 'see the world.' *Really* see it.

Well, she'd seen the world, or Italy, at least, last spring and it hadn't gone so well. "I don't know. My last trip didn't really turn out that great."

"That wasn't a trip," Helen countered. "That was a flight from the police. Hardly a relaxing getaway. You need something to take your mind off...everything." Helen's gaze slipped to the refrigerator where, among the poetry magnets and the half-composed grocery list, were several sketches.

Zoe bit her lip and considered again whether she should let Helen in on her secret. Normally, Zoe shared everything with Helen. It was hard to keep something from the person who knew the name of your secret middle school crush and had not only helped you move into your first apartment, but also commiserated with you, providing dark chocolate and ice cream, during the week of the double-whammy when your boyfriend dumped you *and* your mother announced her engagement to her latest boyfriend, who had been closer to Zoe's age than her mother's age.

Zoe had told Helen everything that had happened during her unexpected trip to Italy. How she'd found out her ex-husband, Jack, hadn't been completely honest about his life prior to their marriage, and how his past had entangled both her and Jack in a series of events, which culminated in a chase from southern Italy to Venice.

The only detail Zoe had left out was about a piece of mail she received after she returned home.

"I know it's been rough these last few months," Helen said.

Zoe nodded. She knew if she opened her mouth, she'd blurt out the whole story. She kept her lips pressed firmly together. She'd kept quiet so long. No use in breaking her silence now. It would only wound Helen to know she'd kept the truth from her this long.

"It's painful, but with Jack..." Helen hesitated, obviously wanting to avoid the word *dead*, "...gone, do you think it would help to clean out the upstairs? I'm here to help. You don't have to do it alone. Just say the word, and I'm here."

"I know." Zoe patted the back of Helen's hand. "I appreciate the offer, but I'm not ready yet."

"Okay. So...the Bahamas," she said with a hopeful inflection. "Sand between our toes. Drinks with little umbrellas. Pool boys to ogle. What do you say?"

Zoe breathed an internal sigh of relief that they weren't talking about Jack. There was only so much deception she could manage with her best friend. "The last thing I want to do is be a third wheel."

"You wouldn't be a third wheel, I promise. It's the annual business conference for Tucker's office. He will be in his panels and meetings all day and half the night. I want someone to hang out on the beach with me."

"You know how I feel about beach vacations. I look like a ghost." Zoe threw out an arm to display her fair skin. Helen was blessed with an olive complexion. After a day in the sun, she'd be a rich, golden tan. Even forty-five minutes in the sun scorched Zoe's skin. Beach and pool time meant floppy hats and layers of sunscreen. "One day on the beach and I'll look like a sunburnt ghost."

"We'll get a cabana. And, there's shopping—the local straw market sounds fun. We can get massages, too."

"I don't think it's a good idea..."

"I think this could be really good for you," Helen said gently. "You're not *you* anymore. I've never understood how you could like living the way you do—flitting from job to job, not having a steady income, but you thrive on it. Or, you did. But ever since Italy, it seems you've lost something...I don't know how to describe it. Passion, maybe. Before, you sparkled with energy. Now, you're like a hermit, shut away in this house, grinding out your freelance work. I understand the whole Italy experience was traumatic, but you've got to move on. And losing Jack...well, I know events change you, but I'm worried about you."

Zoe knew there was a smidge of truth in what Helen said. "I will admit that I was thrown a little...off stride with everything that happened. I have changed some, and I'm trying to get back to normal. I went climbing today." Zoe held up her calloused hands.

Helen rolled her eyes, but smiled. "Great, now you need a manicure. I've got to go. I have a report to finish, but I did pick up sandwiches." She handed Zoe a sub wrapped in white paper. "Turkey for you. I'll have mine at my desk." She buttoned her hound's-tooth jacket and sent Zoe an imploring look. "Please, *please* think about the trip. There's plenty of time to get your passport reissued. I'm sure that FBI agent, the nice one, can help you with that."

"I'll consider it," Zoe said, fingering the edge of the folder where the cotton ball cloud disappeared off the edge. She didn't tell Helen that Mort Vazarri had already greased the wheels of officialdom, and the U.S. government bureaucracy had sent a replacement for the passport she'd lost in the canals of Venice. Her new one was stashed away in her top dresser drawer under a tangle of scarves and belts, but Helen didn't need additional ammunition for her argument, so Zoe simply nodded. "I'll think it over."

"Really?" Helen's raised eyebrows disappeared under her bangs. "Seriously?"

"Yes. I'll *seriously* consider it."

Friday, the second week of November

Cape Town

VICTOR Costa sipped his cappuccino as he studied the view from the hotel balcony. He sat almost motionless, except for the small movement of the cup to his lips, absorbing the heat of the sun on his face and torso like a lizard sunning on a rock. The constant exposure to the sun had lightened his close cropped sandy-colored hair so that the tint of gray was barely noticeable. His flat face, with its thin lips and narrow nose that barely broke the plain of his cheekbones, had tanned and darkened, highlighting his pale gray eyes.

He liked to spend his mornings on the balcony. Table Mountain with its dark gray cliffs rose sharply in the distance, hedging in the city of Cape Town, a jumble of buildings and palm trees, which spread across the valley and down to the waterfront. There was something comforting about the view. The flat, mesa-like mountain looming over the city reminded him of Mt. Vesuvius, and, while the busy city below the mountain wasn't Naples, at least they did know how to make decent coffee.

Heels cracked sharply on the tile floor, then Anna dropped into the seat beside him. "Do you know how hot it is?" she demanded, flicking her head to the side, throwing her long fringe of dark bangs out of her eyes. "Eighty-eight degrees," she said. "In November! At," she paused to consult the diamond-studded watch he had given her, "eight-thirty in the morning."

"In November, it is not warm like this in...Virginia?" he asked. It was a little game they played. When he met her two years ago on a beach on the French Riviera, she had been wearing a slip of fabric shaped into a bikini and had refused to tell him where she was from. Her accent marked her as American, but she wouldn't provide any specifics, saying it was better that way. Of course, Costa had her investigated and knew that Anna Whitmore had grown up in Illinois with two older brothers, had attended college in Washington state, and then worked in computer technology for a firm in California where she had an affair with her married boss. She'd come to the Mediterranean after the boss broke off the affair. When Costa offered her a job, she'd taken it and hadn't returned to the States since.

"No. Wrong again," she said with a smirk then returned to her previous topic. "It shouldn't be this hot so late in the year. It's not right."

"Then you will be glad." He set his cup in the saucer with a click. "We are leaving."

"Now?" She tensed.

"No, there is no rush. Later, this afternoon."

She leaned over the arm of the wicker chair, her delicate

eyebrows drawn tight over her narrowing brown eyes. "Ernesto heard something, didn't he?"

Costa shrugged one shoulder, then waved his hand at the iPad she held in her lap. "*Prego*," he said, indicating he was ready to begin.

The corners of Anna's lips tightened. He could tell she was displeased that he wouldn't say more, but she tapped the screen and went through the business items that needed his attention. He relaxed in the chair, dealing with the issues while he admired the way her skirt molded to her thighs.

"Last thing," she said, consulting the notes on her calendar. "It has been six months since Jack Andrews was seen."

Costa's lazy gaze had been meandering up her hips to the triangle of deep brown skin at the "v" near the collar of her shirt, but at her words, his light gray gaze snapped to her face. "Nothing?"

"No sightings. Not in Italy. Not in the States. He really must be dead."

He turned and stared at the water. "No matter," he said after a moment. "There is still the girl. She will have to do." Costa had waited long enough for this investment to payoff. If Jack Andrews wasn't available to be the scapegoat, his ex-wife would do just as well.

"What would you like me to do?" Anna asked.

"Nothing yet," Costa said. He would take care of it. He would put the plan in motion himself on Monday.

Tuesday, the third week of November

Dallas

ZOE saw the silver car out of the corner of her eye and knew before her careful second glance that it was the same one she'd seen earlier that morning in the parking lot of the grocery store. She forced herself to keep up the same leisurely pace down the driveway. As she opened her mailbox and grabbed the stack of junk mail, she ducked her head and snuck another glance through the curtain of her hair as it fell forward.

Same crack in the upper corner of the windshield. The bright Texas sun, still warm at the peak of the day despite the November date, glinted on the jagged fracture that tilted up and down like a line graph. She paced slowly up the driveway. The papers wrinkled in her tight grip, her heart hammering as if she'd just jogged around the neighborhood.

Zoe slammed the kitchen door behind her, dropped the crumpled flyers on the island, and climbed the stairs two at a time, barely pausing at the top. She hadn't been upstairs in six months, not since she'd returned from her unscheduled trip to Italy last April. At that time, she and Jack had been living in the same house. Their short-lived, impulsive Vegas marriage had fizzled, and they'd divorced, but they couldn't sell the house, so they'd divided it into his and hers sections.

Jack had lived upstairs and survived with a mini-fridge and a hotplate. Zoe had taken the downstairs guest bedroom and used the kitchen island as her freelance office. They had had separate lives: Jack had his start-up business in green energy, GRS Technology, and Zoe had her freelance copy-editing work plus a commercial property management gig and several dog-walking regulars. It had almost been like living in a duplex, minus the dividing wall.

But then Jack's business partner was murdered and Jack had disappeared. Things had gone downhill from there. Hard to imagine it getting worse, but it had. Millions of dollars went missing from GRS accounts and it looked as if not everything in the company had been on the up-and-up. Initially, the police thought Jack was dead, but when his body wasn't discovered, they changed their working theory from "missing, presumed dead," to "alive, presumed involved, if not guilty of murder and theft."

After racing halfway across the country to find answers, Zoe had discovered Jack was alive and that he'd skipped over several not so minor details from his past, including his former employer, the Central Intelligence Agency.

When the dust settled, Jack had been cleared of the murder and the money had been returned to the business account, which was now frozen while the FBI investigated a scam that had been run through GRS. Zoe had last seen Jack diving into a Venice canal in pursuit of the man who murdered his business partner. The other man had been found, but there had been no sign of Jack, dead or otherwise.

For six months.

Except for a sketch that had been mailed to her after she returned from Italy, Zoe hadn't heard anything, but because of the sketch she knew he was out there. She couldn't explain it, not even to Helen. She just *knew* it. She figured he was waiting for the investigation to end. Once his name was cleared of fraud charges, Zoe knew Jack would return. In the meantime, she'd been living in suspended animation, waiting.

And now he had shown up. He must have heard something about the fraud case. Maybe it was closed? Strange that she hadn't heard anything, though.

Jack's room was dusty and she could see the evidence of the police search that had precipitated her flight from Dallas six months ago. Drawers hung open, clothes were scattered over the floor and piled on the bed, and papers tilted in stacks on the small desk in the corner. Zoe hadn't bothered to look around here herself after she returned. Helen had kept an eye on the house and told her that the police had searched first, then the FBI. Zoe had the itemized list of the things they'd taken—Jack's laptop, several boxes of files related to GRS, and, curiously, his four-cup coffeepot. If there was anything interesting to be found, Zoe was sure they would have discovered it.

Zoe twitched back the curtain. Through the bare branches of the cottonwood tree that towered in front of the window, she could see the silver car. It made sense that he'd be cautious. Caution was one of his hallmarks. He'd survey the situation, get the lay of the land. Jack wasn't one to rush into things.

She spotted a shadowy figure in the driver's seat and a smile curled up the corners of her lips. She should be angry, she knew. Six months and not a word. Not a *single* one, but she wasn't mad, not right this second, anyway. Right now, she was relieved.

She'd seen plenty of evidence that Jack could take care of himself, but there had been that niggling worry at the back of her mind, which she'd refused to acknowledge, that something might have happened to him. The figure shifted in the car, and the strong sunlight hit a patch of hair.

Zoe's smile faded. Jack's hair was dark, not light.

———

MORT didn't recognize the number on the display of his office phone. "Special Agent Vazarri," he said, continuing to read the file spread across his desktop. After a second, he looked up. "Come again?"

He swiveled toward his younger partner. Greg Sato was on the phone, too, setting up a dinner date. Sato leaned back in his chair, one elbow propped on the chair arm as he twirled his gold pen through his fingers.

Mort caught Sato's eye and pointed to the phone. "New development. Jack Andrews case."

Sato's feet hit the floor. He ended his call and moved to Mort's desk.

"Are you sure?" Mort asked the caller. "Okay, send me whatever you *do* have." He slapped his phone down and said to Sato, "The money's gone."

Sato's dark eyes narrowed. "How much?"

Mort used the hunt-and-peck method of typing to bring up his email account and log in. "All of it. The GRS account has been cleaned out."

"That's impossible," Sato said. "That account is frozen."

"I know." Mort pushed the monitor so the overhead florescent lights didn't glare on it. "But there it is." He tapped the screen. "Zilch."

Sato whistled. "Computer trail?"

"They're working on it."

Sato leaned against a nearby desk and crossed his arms. "There go your last few weeks. No coasting into retirement now."

Mort shrugged. "Didn't think that would happen anyway." He was scheduled to retire December thirty-first.

Sato pointed his chin at the computer monitor. "How long ago did it go missing?"

"Yesterday. Seven p.m."

"We'd better pay the ex-Mrs. Andrews a visit."

———

THE frigid wind sliced across the back of Anna's neck. She shivered and turned up the collar of her coat. This was more like it. It should be cold during the holidays. She needed to buy a scarf at the market. And gloves, she thought happily, as she cupped her pink fingers around the lighter to protect the flame as she lit a cigarette. Her thick black hair was cut in a severe stacked bob that ended above the nape of her neck. The sides that framed her face were cut on a diagonal, leaving the left side longer than the right. She took a long drag on the cigarette and paced a few steps farther from Ernesto, who was waiting near the car.

They were driving to a nearby city for dinner, and Victor had been held up by a phone call. She ambled a few more feet along the thick stone wall, her boots squishing down into the moist decaying leaves and pine needles that lined the side of the road. She slipped her cell phone out of her pocket, dialed, and placed it to her ear. It rang twice, then Wade answered.

"Are you in position? Were you able to get there?" Anna

asked. It was the first moment she'd had alone since the long flight from South Africa. She glanced over her shoulder. Ernesto stamped his feet by the car door, blowing out clouds of white air. No sign of Victor.

"Course. No probs," said Wade. "So you think this will work? He'll really pay up?"

"Yes, it will work. He needs her to take the fall. Otherwise, it all comes back on him."

"So, when should I do it?"

There was a murmur of voices behind her. She made a show of taking another long drag on the cigarette. She kept the phone hidden under her swath of hair. "Now. Do it now."

She dropped her cigarette and ground it out with the toe of her polished boot while slipping the phone into her pocket.

She turned, climbed the small incline to the car, a smile on her face. "All ready?"

3

It wasn't Jack. Zoe backed away from the window and sat down on the corner of the bed. She'd been so excited, so sure it was Jack.

Maybe her instincts were way off, and he wasn't ever going to show up. She'd thought a lot about Helen's "intervention." Maybe Helen was right and Zoe needed to move on, stop waiting for Jack. He hadn't made any promises, just said that he would see her again and that was vague at best.

This waiting around thing was new for her. Helen had once said Zoe had the attention span of a puppy. She'd been joking, but Zoe knew there was an element of truth in that statement. She constantly shifted things around in her life—whether it was hobbies, boyfriends, or jobs. She'd never liked status quo and made sure her life was always vibrant. At least, that's how Zoe saw it. Helen would say Zoe never finished anything and had zero patience. But she had been content to wait for Jack.

During these last months, she had pictured herself as a

Penelope-like figure, waiting loyally. But at what point did waiting stop being faithful and become pathetic?

There was no guarantee Jack would come back. Even though he had always come through in the past, that didn't mean he would now. Maybe it was time to approach things differently. Zoe wasn't ready to go so far as a beach vacation, but she needed a new perspective, a more realistic perspective.

She looked back to the window. She'd try and sort out those thoughts later. Right now, she needed to figure out why someone had followed her from the grocery store then parked and watched her house. Maybe her past experiences had made her paranoid, but she wanted a closer look at the person in the car.

She stood, pulled her cell phone from the back pocket of her jeans, turned on the camera, and zoomed, but the person had leaned back into the shadows. The image was too fuzzy to distinguish any details.

She pursed her lips to the side, wishing Jack liked to hunt. If he did, he'd have binoculars. Her favorite step-dad, Eric, had been outdoorsy and loved fly-fishing, hunting, and riding horses. There had always been a set of binoculars around the house when Eric had lived with them. Unfortunately, Jack's sports of choice were running and martial arts.

Zoe galloped downstairs to her room and pawed through her dresser until she found her digital camera. Its zoom wasn't much better than the one on her phone, but after she returned upstairs, she did manage to capture two grainy photos of the figure.

She used the review feature on the camera to enlarge the figure. Definitely a man, she decided as she studied the silhouette's broad shoulders. His hair looked blond and a little on the bushy side, but in the shadows she couldn't distinguish anything else. She snapped a wide shot of the car as well then a close-up of the license plate.

Suddenly, she felt a bit silly. What was she doing? It wasn't as though she'd be able to find out who owned the car, and it was probably all a coincidence. People sat in cars on neighborhood streets all the time. He could be waiting for a friend, or maybe he pulled over to make a phone call. Maybe he was lost and reprogramming his GPS. There were a hundred different things he could be doing.

Zoe watched for five more minutes. The car didn't move. She blew out a breath. Well, there was one way to find out if the guy in the silver car was interested in her or if it was a coincidence. She needed to run over to the office park where she owned two business suites and see if a bathroom repair had been completed.

Like all contracting jobs, this one was running behind. So far, the contractor's mom had been hospitalized and his grandmother had died. Zoe was thinking of demanding a note from the doctor and/or priest if anyone else got sick or transitioned to the great beyond.

Originally, her Aunt Amanda, who believed real estate was the only worthwhile investment, had owned the business suites. Zoe had acted as property manager each winter when Aunt Amanda went south to Florida. When Aunt Amanda moved to Sarasota full-time, she gave the properties to Zoe, calling them an early inheritance. Zoe had protested, but her aunt had said, "God knows, my sister will never have anything to leave you, despite her grand plans. Trust me, take the real estate. Diamonds may be a girl's best friend, but real estate ain't bad either."

That had been five years ago, and Zoe had come to agree with her aunt. It was the income from the office suites that had paid the house note during the last six months. Thank goodness she'd been able to rent both offices. A freelance photographer who made realtors and business execs look good in brochures and on billboards occupied one. It was the other office Zoe had been worried about. Infamous death didn't exactly enhance a property's appeal.

But mellow, soft-spoken Sam Clark hadn't minded. Zoe had debated not telling him about the office's somewhat grisly history in order to get it rented, but she couldn't do it.

At their first meeting, when she saw him across the parking lot, she'd assumed he was quite a bit older than she was because of his white hair, but as she closed the distance, she realized he was young, probably no more than thirty with a thick head of dark hair going prematurely white.

He'd been wearing a T-shirt that read, "Music Addict," along with a pair of cargo shorts and thick-soled Newport sandals. A small wooden cross hung from a leather strip around his neck, and several woven bracelets bracketed his diving watch. He ran a business called Encore, which bought and resold used musical instruments. He'd started the business in California, but was expanding to Texas because of the "more favorable business climate," he'd said on the phone when Zoe first talked to him.

As she showed him the office, he hadn't said much, but he'd flashed a smile in her direction a time or two, almost shyly. He moved through the office suite in a patient, methodical way, not saying much. He had a quietness, a self-possessed aura that almost made Zoe nervous. The less he talked, the more she did.

Sam had been pacing off one of the offices when Zoe had finally said, "There was a murder here, in this room...in case that sort of thing bothers you."

Sam paused, ran one hand over the mostly dark stubble that covered his cheeks, as he looked over the room. He nodded a few times, then finally said, "New carpet?"

"Yes," Zoe said, a bit uncertainly. It was the last comment she'd expected.

"And pad?"

Zoe cleared her throat. "Yes. I had the whole thing redone. New paint, carpet, and padding."

His solemn face creased into a smile that reached up to his warm brown eyes. "Just kidding with you there. In general, I find murder unsettling, but I couldn't resist. You looked so worried."

Zoe let out a laugh. "It does make it a hard sell. Anyone who knows about it...well, once they see which office it is, they're out of here."

"It does explain why the price is so good. I need to expand, and it appears this is the only office space in the whole Metroplex that I can afford, so I guess I can't be squeamish."

Zoe angled her head at him as she asked, "You really won't be uncomfortable?"

"No, I'm not superstitious, and since this seems to be a gang-free part of the city, I'm assuming that it wasn't a drive-by shooting. The likelihood of it being repeated is low?"

"Minuscule. Non-existent, in fact. It was a situation related to the former occupants and that's over," Zoe said, feeling only a tad guilty for not mentioning that her ex-husband had been one of the prior tenants and the fraud case was still under investigation, but she shook it off. He didn't need to know that detail.

He'd moved in the next week, paid his rent on time, and never complained. So when he called and said there was a water leak in the bathroom, Zoe had immediately called in a plumber and had it fixed. The repair hadn't taken long; it was retiling the back wall that was dragging on forever. Zoe wanted to keep Sam happy, and if that meant she had to get in there and tile the back wall of the bathroom herself, she'd do it.

She retraced her steps downstairs, wound a lightweight yellow scarf around her neck, and gathered her sunglasses and the new leather messenger bag that she'd bought after returning home from Italy. Her old bag hadn't survived the trip. Her new one wasn't broken in and didn't have the worn patina of the original, but she was working on it. She normally didn't spend much money on clothes or accessories as her no name blue-and-white striped shirt and jeans showed. But the messenger bag was essential, a business expense she reasoned when she shelled out the money for it. It would last for years—as long as she kept it away from Venetian canals.

Fortunately, she and Helen were close to the same size, and Helen was a clotheshorse. Zoe happily recycled Helen's cast-offs, especially enjoying the shoes, like today's calf-length low-heeled boots in nut brown. It really wasn't cold enough for boots, but Zoe couldn't resist wearing them. The first break of the season-long humidity called for a celebration and wearing boots seemed exactly the right way to mark the occasion.

Zoe stepped outside, appreciating the deliciously crisp air as only someone who had lived through the muggy heat of a Dallas summer could. Her phone rang as she walked to the car. Her mother. She considered not answering it, but while calls from her mother were rare, when Donna decided it was time for a chat she was as persistent and focused as one of the dogs Zoe walked regularly, a toy poodle named Lulu, who strained on the leash all the way around the block. Lulu had no idea where she was going, but she was determined to get there as soon as possible.

"Hi, Mom," Zoe said as she slid into her Jetta and slammed the door. "Can't talk long, I'm on my way to the office suites." It was always good to establish her escape route upfront. It lowered expectations for a long chat.

"Darling! You picked up." Donna's husky voice managed to sound both surprised and accusing at the same time. "It doesn't matter if you don't have a lot of time. I'm only in town for a few hours anyway."

Zoe had backed out of the driveway and was keeping an eye on the rearview mirror to see if the silver car followed her, but at her mother's words, she forgot to watch the mirror. "You're here? In Dallas?" Had her mom arrived, intending to spend Thanksgiving with her? No, surely not. Donna hated Thanksgiving. Staying a size two was one of the main focuses of her life. She didn't enjoy any activity or holiday centered around food. When Zoe was a kid, they'd either ignored Thanksgiving Day all together, or she and her current step-dad had take-out from the grocery store deli while Donna nibbled on a salad.

"Yes, that's what I said. Now, I'll wait for you at baggage claim D16."

"Are you here for an audition?" Since abandoning Dallas for Southern California the day after Zoe's high school graduation, Donna hadn't returned for a visit. Zoe had a horrible thought. Tryouts for the Dallas Cowboys cheerleaders weren't this week, were they? Surely not. Wrong season. Please be the wrong season.

"No," Donna said, her voice thick with amusement. "No one auditions in Dallas. At least, not for anything significant. I'm on a layover. My plane for New York leaves at five."

Zoe suddenly remembered the silver car and checked her mirrors, afraid she'd missed seeing whether or not it followed her, but there it was, moving along in the wake of a cream-colored SUV two cars back.

"Baggage Claim, D16," Donna repeated. "I suppose you still have that rickety little car?"

"I'll be in the Jetta, yes."

"Too bad I don't have time to rent a limo," Donna said under her breath.

Zoe adjusted her driving plan in her mind. Driving to the airport would take her away from the office suites, but it would certainly make it clear if the silver car was interested in her or if it was simply a coincidence that it had followed her route.

"I'll see you in about thirty minutes," Zoe said and quickly hung up before her mom could make some convoluted plan like renting a stretch Hummer limo—probably in hot pink—on a whim.

4

Zoe checked the mirror and saw the glint of the silver car behind her. It followed her up the entrance ramp to the Tollway. The caravan of cars she was part of merged onto the larger road, and the mass of cars on the Tollway engulfed the line of cars. She lost the silver car. She drove for a while and didn't see it. She was telling herself she'd become far too paranoid when she saw it one lane over. It was almost in her blind spot. Maybe it was another silver car? She did a head check. Sunlight glinted on the jagged crack.

Maybe it was just a coincidence? Maybe the person driving the silver car happened to be in her neighborhood today and then needed to run to the airport, too? The road forked ahead, the left road continued south while the right road bent to the west toward Lewisville. She signaled and moved into the left-hand lane. The silver car dropped back, then merged into the same lane behind a black Suburban and followed her as she took the left fork. Zoe bit her lip as a couple more exits whizzed by.

The exit for the Stemmons Freeway, an interstate that sliced through central Dallas on a diagonal, was next. She shifted to the far right-hand lane and the silver car stuck with her like a distant shadow. Despite it being daylight and being surrounded with commuters, she was getting a tad freaked out. What would happen when she got to the airport? Would the driver get out and follow her inside? Confront her? Or, just keep following her at a distance?

Zoe took the double-lane exit ramp for south Stemmons in the far right-hand lane. The silver car followed her. The two lanes began to peel off of the Tollway. She checked over her left shoulder. There was a gap in the cars. She bit her lip, waited until the last possible second then pulled the wheel hard to the left.

With her shoulders hunched up around her ears, the Jetta threaded the needle between two cars. Horns blared as she swept across the wide white lines that marked the dividing point between the exit and the Tollway.

Heart pounding, she rocked into an open slot on the Tollway then quickly glanced over her shoulder and saw the silver car's back end pop up as the driver hit the brakes. He wanted to follow Zoe across the lanes, but there was too much traffic. He was blocked in. Like a bit of wood caught in the current of a stream, Zoe watched as the car sailed along the exit lane, which swept up and then curved back toward her as it arched over the Tollway.

Zoe tightened her fingers on the steering wheel as she drove under the bridge and tried to get her breathing under control. *Okay, I'm not imagining things*, she thought. *He definitely was following me.*

She mentally reviewed the roads. There was no way the

driver of the silver car could catch up to her. There was no quick shortcut back to the Tollway, and it would take the driver forever to get off at the next exit and work his way back to the interchange. Still, she didn't want to linger. She pressed the accelerator down and hoped that there were no traffic police lurking about.

IT wasn't hard for Zoe to find her mom. She was the only woman in a full-length white wool coat with a furry collar and Ugg boots standing outside one of the doorways to baggage claim. She flicked her head around so that the wind would pull the long strands of her mahogany hair out of her face and took a long drag on her cigarette, then stubbed it out.

Zoe waved as she closed the distance. "Hello, Mom."

"Darling!" Donna deposited air kisses on each side of Zoe's face then said, "Donna. Call me Donna." She pulled away and shot a quick glance around the sidewalk to see if anyone had heard Zoe drop the 'm' word.

"It's okay," Zoe said. "DFW isn't a big paparazzi hang out."

"You never know," Donna said, her voice lilting with hope. She reached forward and pinched some of Zoe's hair, examining it. "Your hair. It's still red. I thought you said you dyed it a nice brown," she said, clearly disappointed.

"It was a rinse, Mom. It washed out." Donna had never been pleased with Zoe's red hair. It had only taken Zoe about fifteen years to comprehend that Donna didn't like anything that drew attention away from her. "Well, you could always do it again. Keep things fresh." She threaded her arm through

Zoe's and pointed them to the parking lot. "Now, where's your car? I'm staved."

"We better eat here. You've only got about an hour, and then you'll need to get back through security."

Donna's collagen-enhanced lower lip pouted. "Are you sure there isn't somewhere close? I was hoping for a cute little bistro."

"Afraid not." Zoe steered her mom inside the doors. If there was one thing Zoe was sure of, it was that they weren't taking a chance on getting caught in a Dallas traffic jam. She wanted to make sure Donna made that flight. The thought of dealing with strange people in silver cars following her paled in comparison to the thought of an unscheduled visit from her mom.

They found a little sandwich shop and settled into a table that Donna picked near the front of the restaurant, clearly hoping that someone would recognize them and ask for an autograph. They quickly covered the topic of Zoe's "little editing job," then Donna asked, "Anything else going on? All of that horrid GRS stuff has been resolved?"

"Yes, that's all over." Zoe had no compunction about keeping the truth from her mom. If Donna knew the truth, that Jack was still alive, she'd be texting *Entertainment Tonight* faster than she ran down the aisle to get married.

"How long will you be in New York? Are you coming back through Dallas for Thanksgiving?"

"No, I'm staying in New York to shop. I have my meeting tomorrow, then a spa day on Thursday."

"You found a spa that's open on Thanksgiving?"

"New York is an international city. Not everyone cele-brates Thanksgiving."

Zoe was having a turkey and ham sandwich with chips on the side and noticed that Donna was staring at the chips with an almost longing expression. "Want some?" Zoe asked, swiveling the plate toward Donna.

"No. They're carbs." Her red-tipped fingernails traced across her flat abdomen. She flicked a crouton to the side of her salad and pierced several pieces of Romaine.

"So what's new with you?" Zoe asked, then shot a quick glance at Donna's left hand and saw with relief that it was bare. Zoe had hurried into marriage with Jack, but at least she'd only married hastily once. Donna was up to five marriages and an equal number of divorces.

She crunched through the lettuce then said, "I've been asked to be a special features correspondent for one of the morning shows. I'm on my way to New York to meet the producer."

"A local New York show?"

"No. *Daybreak*."

Zoe sat back, stunned. *Daybreak* was a national network morning show. "Wow, that's great."

"I know." Donna pushed away her still-full salad bowl. "It's a wonderful opportunity. I'll travel the country, do interviews, and have three in-studio appearances a month."

"So you're auditioning for it?"

"No, it's a done deal. They want me to start next month."

"They know you don't have any reporting experience, right?"

Donna waved a hand through the air. "Nothing to worry about. The producer will do all that kind of thing...the detail work." She fiddled with her fork. "There's only one tiny drawback." Donna leaned forward and whispered, "It's for their

retirement lifestyle correspondent. I'm not retired. I'm not a
senior," she hissed and glanced around as if she'd said a
dirty word.

"No...but you're close."

Donna's carefully sculpted eyebrows shot upward. "I'm
barely in my forties."

Zoe knew *Donna* was teetering on the brink of the big
five-oh, but she didn't contradict her. Instead, she did some
damage control. "You know how it is in TV—everything
skews younger."

"Well, that is true," Donna said, mollified.

"You should definitely go check it out. Sounds like a good
opportunity."

"Yes, I know," she said, nodding her head. "It would keep
me out there. Exposure is everything now with the media so
fractured."

Relieved that her mom's trip to Dallas was nothing to do
with the cheerleaders or announcing nuptials, Zoe finished
off her sandwich and checked her watch. "You better get
going. The security lines look pretty long," Zoe said.

"Already? Well, you're probably right." She stood, struggled into her coat with the enormous furry collar. They
exchanged another set of air kisses, and Zoe walked with her
out of the restaurant.

"Oh! I almost forgot. This came in the mail for you."
Donna pulled a small package from her leather handbag and
gave it to Zoe.

There was no return address on the brown box, only a
smudged postmark. It was addressed to Zoe care of Donna's
Los Angeles address. The address was in Times New Roman

font on a piece of printer paper that had been taped to the front.

"It didn't look like the usual junk mail I get in your name."

"You get junk mail addressed to me?"

"Sure, all the time. Mostly, from that college you attended for a couple of years. They want you to donate to their alumni group or some silly thing like that. I just throw it away. Good-bye, darling! I'm off to New York, New York!" she said, flinging out her hand and doing a little dance step as she moved away.

"Bye. Good luck," Zoe called as she wrenched the tape away and opened the box. At first glance, it appeared empty, but when she flexed the flaps open wider and tilted it over her hand, a princess-cut diamond ring on a gold chain dropped into her palm.

5

I t was her wedding ring, the ring that Jack had insisted she keep after their divorce, the ring that should either be at the bottom of a Venetian canal or in an evidence locker with the Italian police. "Well, this is ironic," Zoe whispered as she turned the ring around in her fingers. It showed up on the very day she'd considered—for the first time—the possibility that Jack might not come back.

A slip of pale blue paper had followed the ring out of the box and had floated lazily to the floor. Zoe snatched up the paper and ran after her mother. She caught up with her as she balanced on one foot, pulling off an Ugg boot. "Mom, how long have you had this?" Zoe asked, holding up the box. She held the ring in the tightly closed fist of her other hand.

"Donna," she said, patting Zoe's cheek. "It's Donna." She was smiling, but Zoe could see her back teeth were clamped together.

"How long have you had this, Donna?"

"Oh, I don't know. A few weeks? Maybe a month or two? I

kept meaning to mail it to you and forgot, but when I saw it on my way out the door today, I thought I'll just take this with me," she said in an aren't-I-clever tone. "Oh, must move on."

They went through the air kiss routine again, but Zoe was barely aware of it. She returned Donna's final wave before she disappeared into the line for the scanners, but she was thinking about the ring. She'd asked about it, if it had been recovered, but was told that it hadn't been found.

The sharp edges of the diamond cut into her palm. Someone had clearly found it, and she suspected it was Jack. But how would he get it? And why would he mail it to Donna? Donna, of all people! It was a miracle she hadn't trashed it with the junk mail. And it was a good thing she'd never opened it. If she had, Zoe had no doubt the ring would have gone on Donna's finger, and she would conveniently forget the box had been addressed to Zoe. Shiny things had a tendency to mesmerize Donna.

Zoe examined the ring again. It was definitely hers. She recognized the long gold chain threaded through the ring. Her initials, along with Jack's, were engraved inside.

"Please move along, ma'am." Zoe looked up to find a TSA official waving her into the line for security.

Zoe stepped backward. "Sorry. I'm not traveling." She slipped the necklace over her head, letting the ring settle under her neckline. She examined the box as she walked through the airport. The postage date was smeared, but readable. June. It had been mailed in June. Zoe walked faster, a spurt of anger surging through her. She didn't know how long it would take something to go from—she consulted the postmark again and halted as she made out the words, "Royal Mail" and "London."

London? Was Jack in London? That didn't make sense. As far as she knew, Jack had never been there. But, then again, there were a lot of things that she hadn't known about Jack.

She examined the blue slip of paper, which contained a string of ten numbers interspersed with dots. She flipped it over. A skull and crossbones sketch filled the other side.

Well, that was cryptic. Was Jack trying to tell her he was in trouble? She went back to the numbers and frowned. Maybe it was a phone number and Jack had thrown the dots in there to disguise it? But why wouldn't he just write the phone number down the normal way with dashes? She tapped the number into her phone and got a recording telling her the number wasn't in service.

She rubbed the paper between her fingers, feeling frustrated. Would it kill him to write her a note, using actual words? No room for misunderstanding there. She sighed. She'd been through this before. Last spring when her normal world disintegrated, there had been mysterious numbers and every thought she'd had about them had been wrong. She sifted through the possibilities for this string of numbers: bank account, lock combination, dates. Heck, they could even be GPS coordinates. How many digits did GPS locations have? She'd have to find out, Zoe decided. If the numbers were supposed to mean something to her, she was clueless. She tucked the paper into the box and headed to her car.

She was still thinking about the numbers on the blue paper when she arrived at the office suite. She waved to Al, the teen who worked for Sam part-time. "Is Sam in?" Zoe asked.

"Nope." He always looked a little anemic, but today he looked as if he was on the verge of hospitalization. His black

T-shirt with the words, "Anarchists Unite," contrasted sharply with his pale skin. His long brown hair was parted down the middle of his head and drawn back into a ponytail at the nape of his neck showing off his single small hoop in one earlobe. Zoe had once spent a painful fifteen minutes in attempted chitchat with him while she waited for Sam to show up. Unable to get more than ten words out of Al, she'd said, "You're not much of a talker, are you?" He'd solemnly replied, "I let my music speak for me."

"I'm here to check the repairs," she said. "Interesting shirt," she called over her shoulder.

"It's ironic," Al said, deadpan.

"Okay." She wasn't sure if he was serious or joking. She entered the bathroom and nearly fainted. Could it be? The repair was actually finished? No, she wasn't imagining things. The job was done. She gave the tiles a close inspection. They looked great. A chime sounded, indicating the front door had opened. Zoe stepped into the reception area. Sam closed the front door as he tossed a set of keys to Al and said, "Thanks."

Al caught them. "Sure, man."

"Good news," Zoe said, and Sam turned to her quickly, clearly surprised to find her in the office. "Sorry. Didn't mean to startle you. I was here to check the repair. After only four weeks—it's done."

"That is too bad," Sam said. He had on a white oxford shirt with the cuffs rolled up and a pair of jeans. He was still sporting the stubble look, but on him it didn't come off as sloppy as if he'd simply put off shaving.

"Why is that bad?" Zoe asked. Had the repairman slacked off and she missed it?

Sam's gaze was on a stack of messages he'd picked up.

"That means no more unexpected visits from my landlady." Head bent over the messages, he glanced up at her with a little smile.

Was he flirting with her? Zoe toyed with the set of keys Al had placed on the counter, fingering the leather fob imprinted with the letters *O* and *B*. "Oh. Well. I was just trying to stay on top of things."

Sam put down the messages. "That's good. To stay on top of...things."

Were they even talking about repairs? Zoe felt a blush creeping into her cheeks as his smile widened. He was *flirting* with her. She was flattered. He was an attractive man, after all. But there was Jack, always in the back of her mind. Of course, Jack wasn't here—hadn't been here in months.

"Since the slow repairman is finally finished, I may have to resort to taking you out for a coffee to see you?" He put an inflection on the end of the sentence and raised his eyebrows slightly.

She almost said no, but then thought of her disappointment this morning when she realized Jack wasn't about to walk in the door. No guarantees, she reminded herself. New perspective. "Sure."

It was just coffee, after all.

ZOE was thinking more about Sam than about the silver car when she drove home, but as soon as she turned into her neighborhood, she scanned the cars on her block. No silver car. It probably hadn't been the smartest thing to give the silver car the slip this morning, Zoe thought. It certainly wouldn't be hard to find her again. It wasn't as if the driver didn't know where she lived.

As she cruised down her street, she did see a familiar car, a brown four-door sedan with special plates. "Oh, no," Zoe groaned, wanting to slip past her driveway and keep moving, but they'd seen her. She'd spotted the tall guy in the driver's seat with the dark hair. That would be Special Agent Sato. He made eye contact with her as she closed the distance, and she bet that he was putting his car in DRIVE in case Zoe decided not to stop. There had been that little incident when she slipped out from under his nose last time. She was sure he wasn't about to let it happen again. The front fender of his car edged into the street as if to block her.

Zoe sighed and pulled into her driveway. She parked and walked back from the garage, knowing that she wouldn't have seriously attempted to escape Sato. It would have been entertaining, but she was sure this was another of the occasional visits the FBI paid her. They liked to keep in touch. At least Sato's partner Mort—he'd asked her to call him that, but it still felt weird—was nice and didn't have her penciled in as "guilty."

She met them at the mailbox. Sato nodded at her, hand skimming down his fuchsia silk tie. "Afternoon, Ms. Hunter. We have a few questions for you."

"All right," she said, hoping she appeared calm and unruffled. On the inside, her thoughts were racing. Sato had once insinuated that Jack might not be dead, that he might have conveniently disappeared. Had they somehow found out about the ring? Maybe the guy in the silver car had been from the FBI? But how could they know about the ring? She'd lost the guy in the silver car before she got to the airport. She knew Sato and Mort weren't at the airport themselves. They were quite a pair and would have stood out, even among the crowds.

Sato moved impatiently toward the house, looking like a bad-tempered menswear model who'd stepped out of a Giorgio Armani ad. Mort, on the other hand, with his unruly thatch of gray hair, barrel-chest, and wrinkled gray dress shirt, had a more neutral expression. Zoe wondered again how they managed to work together. They seemed to be opposites not only in appearance, but also in personality. Sato was smooth with slicked back black hair, suave innuendo, and designer suits while Mort was rumpled and comfortably straightforward.

Zoe asked, "What is this about?"

"Let's talk inside, if you don't mind," Mort said, and Zoe noticed a trace of formality in Mort's tone that wasn't usually there. It worried her.

She led them through the garage and into the kitchen where she flicked on the lights, dumped her stuff on the counter beside the sink, and gestured for them to take a seat at the barstools at the island. Sato pulled out a barstool, but Mort wandered to the other side of the kitchen and leaned against the counter, eyeing the missing drywall above his head.

"Something to drink?" she asked, reaching for glasses, which gave her something to do with her jittery hands. Even if they did know about the ring, there was no actual connection to Jack, Zoe reminded herself. She suspected it was from him, but she had no proof. "I've got ice tea or water."

Sato shook his head, but Mort accepted a glass of water. Zoe filled one for herself, then dragged one barstool around to the other side of the large island and sat down opposite Sato.

"Where's the money?" Sato asked.

The question was so different from what she expected. "What money?"

"The money that was in the GRS business account, the money that was obtained by fraudulent means."

"The money in the frozen account?" Zoe asked, glad that the question was about Jack's old business account and not about his whereabouts or if he'd contacted her. "In the account, I assume."

"Is that the way you want to play it? Total denial?" Sato removed a notepad and gold pen from his jacket.

Zoe had taken a sip of her water. She set her glass down slowly. His accusing tone set off alarm bells. "What are you saying? That it's not there? It's missing...*again*?"

"Yes," Sato said.

Zoe glanced at Mort, who was sipping his water and studying her from across the room with what looked like a trace of disappointment in his gaze.

"Well, I had nothing to do with it. I have no idea where it is. How can that be anyway? I thought you said the account was frozen."

"It was." Sato tapped his pen on the blank page as he stared at her, waiting for a response.

"Why are you looking at me like that? I don't know anything about high finance stuff. I can't unfreeze bank accounts and move funds around." He didn't look convinced, and Zoe's heart began to pump. "I could barely get my own online banking account set up. Here," she said and pulled her laptop across the island. "You can check my bank account—"

Sato interrupted her as he consulted a page in his notepad. "We already have. Four-hundred-eighty-two dollars and nineteen cents."

"See. That's certainly not twelve million dollars."

"What other bank accounts do you have? Anything offshore?"

If the situation hadn't been so absurd, Zoe would have laughed, but she couldn't. She was trying too hard to calm her racing heartbeat. "Do I look like the kind of person who has a bank account on some tropical island? These are not designer clothes—well, except for the boots, and they're hand-me-downs from my friend. Would I have that," she asked, pointing to the hole in the ceiling, "if I had twelve million dollars?" Sato and Mort exchanged a glance. Mort raised his eyebrows and gave a little nod, like he agreed. Satos' face didn't change.

"So you're saying you don't know how the money was moved, and you don't have it," Sato asked, disbelief heavy in his tone.

"Yes, exactly." Zoe took a quick gulp of her water, feeling a bit better as it seemed at least Mort was leaning toward believing her. "So you're saying that you don't have any idea where it is? Can't you track it?" she asked quickly before Sato could ask her any more questions.

Sato flipped his notepad closed and stood up. "We'll know soon enough."

"That's great. Then you can call off your guy in the silver car." They must have sent someone over to watch her house as soon as they found out about the missing money, Zoe thought.

"What guy in the silver car?" Sato asked.

6

"The one who followed me," Zoe said. "He was with you, right? You sent someone to watch me until you could get here."

Mort stepped forward and placed his empty glass on the island. "The car was silver, you said?"

"Yes. He followed me home from the grocery store then parked on the street and watched the house."

"Probably coincidence." Sato transferred Mort's glass to the sink, clearly ready to leave.

"Pretty odd that he'd follow me to the airport today, too."

Sato went back on full alert. "You went to the airport?"

"Yes. My mom had a layover, and I met her for lunch." Zoe forced herself to keep her hands resting on the island even though she had the urge to touch the gold chain around her neck.

"Did he follow you all the way to the airport and back home again?" Sato asked.

"No. I lost him in traffic on the Tollway."

One corner of Mort's mouth turned up. "He probably didn't realize what an...evasive driver you are."

Zoe knew he was thinking of the time she'd given them the slip. Sato had been driving. "Evasive driving is a skill you have to have to survive in Dallas," Zoe said, and Sato made a rumbling sound.

"It was a man? Are you sure?" Mort asked easily, ignoring Sato.

"Yes. In fact—" Zoe retrieved the camera from the hall where she'd left it. "I took a picture." She felt Sato's gaze intensify and she said quickly, "It seemed...weird. And, after everything that happened last time, I wanted a record, just in case I had to prove what I saw." She swiveled the screen on the camera toward Mort. He put on a pair of half-glasses, studied it, and then passed it to Sato. "It was a guy. I could tell by the build. And he had blond hair. That's really all I could tell."

Sato fiddled with the camera, zooming in on the image of the car. "Too blurry to see the plate, but email it to me and I'll send it to our tech..."

He trailed off as Zoe took the camera and moved to the next picture, a close-up of the license plate. Mort took out his phone, adjusted his glasses, and began tapping away.

"You're sure he wasn't from your office?" Zoe asked again.

"Yes. Probably a coincidence," Sato said. "A neighbor going in the same direction as you."

"No one on this block has a car like that," Zoe said.

Sato moved to the door. "Someone probably got a new car."

Mort held up his hand. "Let's just wait a minute, see if Henry texts me."

Sato clearly didn't want to stay another minute. Zoe didn't want them to, either. Her palms went sweaty at the thought of trying to make small talk with these guys.

Fortunately, Mort's phone dinged with a message, and he read aloud, "That car, a silver Camry, is registered to a Martha Baumkirchner. Lives in Farmers Branch." Zoe couldn't help shooting a triumphant glance at Sato as Mort did some more tapping.

"Could it have been stolen?" Zoe asked. She was surprised that Mort had done the search and told her the results.

"It's possible." Mort folded his glasses and tucked them into his breast pocket.

"We'll look into it," Sato said, grudgingly, already on his way out the door.

"Call us, if you see it again," Mort said, leaving his card with her.

———

"So what's your take?" Sato asked as their car doors slammed closed.

Mort snapped his seatbelt. "She seemed to be telling the truth. She's not living like she's got millions stashed away. The ceiling needs a repair. Her laptop is older than mine, and her car certainly isn't new. Bank balance is low."

Sato pulled away from the curb. "I don't know. Maybe she's smart enough to know not to flaunt it. Sure, her bank balance is under five hundred bucks, but maybe she's got the money stashed in some other account, and she's charging up her credit cards."

Mort pulled the thick file out that he'd brought with him. "I checked. Three cards. Zero balance on two. Seventy-four dollars on the other as of yesterday." Mort liked tangible evidence: facts and figures, the hard details that couldn't be argued away or discounted by slick lawyers.

Sato, on the other hand, gravitated to the intangibles: relationships, undercurrents, and motivations. "But there was something, something about the mention of the airport that bothered her. Did you notice her tense up? Wonder what happened at DFW."

"We can check with the airport, see if she's on the their CCTV," Mort said.

AS soon as they were gone, Zoe locked the door then sagged against it. The money was gone. She rubbed her hand across her forehead. The silver car worried her—she had been followed, no matter what Sato thought—but the missing money was even more troubling. Banking errors didn't happen twice, at least not involving twelve million dollars.

With the strange guy following her, the ring showing up, and the money disappearing, it felt as if the situation was heating up again. It had cooled down for a few months, but now things were simmering.

The whole money aspect was beyond her. She didn't have any clue about how to move funds around or figure out who had done it. She was sure the FBI was tracking the money. However, she did have something new to put in her file.

She pushed away from the door and moved to the shelves at the end of the island. She reached behind the row of cookbooks and removed a file folder. In the first months after her return from Italy, she'd researched everything she could find related to Jack's situation. The file contained her clippings from the local newspaper as well as from her Internet searches, everything she could find related to the "Italy Incident," as she had begun to call it. She had articles on Jack, on the scam that had taken in Jack and hundreds of other people, on the investigation, and on Victor Costa. Interestingly, articles about Costa, a powerful player in the *Camorra*, the Naples mafia, made up the bulk of the file.

Jack had never met him. But during the time Jack had worked for the State Department at the Consulate in Naples, Jack had recruited Victor's wife as a source. An asset, Jack had called her. Things went horribly wrong, and Francesca was killed after it was discovered she was informing on her husband. At least, that's what Jack thought had happened. Jack and Zoe hadn't worked out a few extra details until they untied all the convoluted knots in Venice.

Initially, when everything went wrong last spring, Jack suspected Costa was at the heart of it, but several people Jack trusted told him that Costa was in hiding and that he'd essentially retired. Despite the pursuit of several different police forces, including Interpol, Costa hadn't been found. Clearly, not for lack of trying, as the Google news alerts showed. The mention of his name had become more frequent in the last few months.

Zoe settled on the barstool and flipped open the file. She taped the blue slip of paper to the interior of the folder. Unless Jack had suddenly decided to take up pirating, the skull and crossbones had to mean danger. She ran her finger across the tape, considering what the numbers could be, since they weren't a phone number. A code of some sort? But if it were a code, there would have to be a key, a way to decipher it. The paper and the ring had been the only things in the box.

Just to be sure, she double-checked the box, even slitting all the flaps and opening it completely, but it was empty. She pried up the stamp and examined the back. Nothing but adhesive. She frowned at the box, which was now splayed open on the island, like a weird dissection in a biology class.

Okay, what else? Earlier today, she'd thought it could be an account number, like a bank account, but just an account number wouldn't do her any good. She needed at least a hint —a bank name or address. She mentally left "account number" on her list of possibilities then ran through other options. GPS coordinates? She turned on her computer to do a search.

Because it was practically an antique, it took a while for the computer to chug through its opening sequence. While she waited, Zoe paged through the file of articles, noticing that Jenny Singletarry, a reporter for a Dallas newspaper who had been instrumental in breaking the story about GRS, had apparently gone out on her own and now wrote only for her blog, *The Informationalist*, which had a mix of hard news and local entertainment reviews. Jenny had contacted her several times, asking for an interview after Zoe returned from Italy, but Zoe had turned her down. There was no way she was giving information to the media.

Zoe was deep into the stack when an article, this one from a British news website, caught her eye. She'd printed it two months ago because it mentioned Costa, but hadn't read the whole thing at the time, just skimmed it. The headline read,

"Cyber Crime Gets Organized." A photo she'd seen before in other articles was set into the text. The cutline under a fuzzy picture of Costa noted the photo was the last sighting of him.

Striding up a busy street, threading between mopeds and pedestrians, Costa looked to be in his late forties or early fifties, but there was no middle-age spread on him. His suit fit snuggly on his lean frame as he threw a cocky grin at the camera.

Zoe scanned the article. After making a fortune in the chaos following the fracture of the *Camorra* into several warring elements in the early 2000s, Costa disappeared, and investigators believed he'd abandoned drug trafficking and turned to cyber crime. "Cyber crime is difficult to trace and highly mobile," she read. "In the past, cyber crime was often committed by individuals acting alone, but now organized crime syndicates are getting involved and moving the schemes to a whole new level." Zoe's gaze snagged on one paragraph, which read, "Costa was believed to be involved in a virtual theft of millions of dollars from banks throughout Europe. 'It's the new frontier for the mafia,' said the leading expert on Victor Costa's new criminal enterprise, a London-based computer crime consultant, Dave Bent."

Zoe dropped the article onto the stack. The phrase "virtual theft of millions," echoed in her head. Cyber crime would be the perfect activity for a man in hiding. Was Costa really out of the picture? It didn't sound like these experts thought he was retired.

Her computer finally came up, so she opened a browser window and went back to trying to decipher the numbers on the blue paper. She looked up information on GPS coordinates, which torpedoed that idea pretty quickly. She needed

two sets of numbers, latitude and longitude, for an exact location. She cringed, thinking that her seventh grade geography
teacher, Mrs. Roberts, would have been ashamed that she'd
forgotten such a basic fact.

So, it wasn't a geographic location or a phone number. If
it was an account number, she didn't have enough information to make it useful. She swiveled her legs from side to side
on the barstool, thinking that if Jack had sent the ring—and
she thought it was from him—and he'd taken the trouble to
put the paper in the box, he wouldn't send something that
she couldn't figure out. She couldn't picture him sending a
second package with the key to the code. And, God knows, if
he depended on Donna to get a second package to her, they
were sunk. Donna had barely managed to get the ring to her.

No, the more she thought about it, the more she believed
the answer had to be right here in front of her, in the number.
At first, she'd thought the dots were to disguise a phone
number, but since it wasn't a phone number, then maybe the
dots needed to be there. What items used strings of numbers
separated by dots?

Too many dots to be a library call number. She stopped in
mid-swivel and typed the numbers directly into the address
bar on the browser. She'd thought of one of her dog-walking
clients, a free-lance web designer, who had a personalized
welcome mat at his house with his web address—not the
name of his websites, but the digital name—a line of
numbers separated by dots.

She hit return and a page about Covent Garden loaded. A
photo of the popular shopping area filled the top of the
screen along with a description of the area, which had once
been a fruit and vegetable market. Zoe was familiar with

Covent Garden from her guidebook copy-editing and knew it was a popular tourist venue with shops, restaurants, and performers. She quickly skimmed the rest of the website. What was Jack trying to tell her? Was there something in one of these pictures, or in the text she should recognize? Was he at Covent Garden? Or, had he been there when he sent the package?

It was a massive website, providing details on the history, the architecture, upcoming events, and hotels and services in the surrounding areas. Maybe she was completely wrong and the webpage was a coincidence. But there was the London postmark, too...

After studying page after page of shops and restaurants, she pushed away from the computer. She hadn't seen anything that she could even remotely link to Jack. She needed a break. She changed into her running clothes, laced up her Asics, and pulled her hair up into a ponytail.

She set off at a brisk walk to warm-up, enjoying the fact that she didn't have to wait until almost twilight to run, which is what she did during most of the summer. The humidity never really went away in the summer, but it did lessen a little in the late evening. She checked her street and didn't see either a strange silver car driven by an unknown driver or the equally disconcerting brown car driven by the FBI guys. She set off on her usual jog—a three-mile loop through the neighborhood, which was quiet in the early afternoon. It was the lull before the carpool moms hit the road for afternoon pick-up and commuters were still trapped at their desks.

About a mile in, she realized a car was closing in on her from behind.

7

*Z*oe heard the engine and moved farther toward the side of the street. She didn't like to run on the sidewalk because of the driveways. All that up and down messed with her pace, so she ran at the edge of the street, practically in the gutter.

She flicked a glance over her shoulder and saw it was a van. Not a suburban mom with a minivan, but a boxy utilitarian van contractors favored. The van came even with her, hugging the gutter. There was plenty of space for it to get around her. There wasn't another car on the road, and there was no need for it to squeeze so tightly next to her.

She skipped up on the sidewalk and continued running at her regular speed. The van paced her for a moment, which wasn't that usual. The neighborhood was notorious for its frequent police patrols that encouraged drivers to keep their speed down, but when Zoe glanced to the side and made eye contact with the driver, she involuntarily slowed down. He had a shaved head and a low dark unibrow. He stared at her, sparing only a quick look at the road ahead to make sure no one was coming. Zoe felt a shiver of cold anxiety, despite the layer of sweat on her body.

The van sped up, then veered into the driveway of the house in front of her with a screech of brakes, cutting her off.

She halted. Her thoughts leapt to those news stories about women who had been attacked, abducted...horrible things. But that couldn't be happening, not now. Not to her. She wanted to turn around and run in the opposite direction, but that would look silly—like she was afraid. The driver was probably turning around. He'd back out in a second...

The panel door slid open and a second guy, this one tall and stocky, hopped out, his gaze fixed on her. He was several feet away, but another cold wash of fear blanked out every thought. She went with her instinct—run.

Zoe turned and sprinted back the way she'd come. She ran as hard as she had ever run, adrenaline making her fast and nimble. She ducked under a low-hanging tree branch and swooshed by a set of low hedges, their stiff leaves scraping her legs, but she barely noticed.

She twisted her head to look behind her, expecting to see the guy chasing her, but he'd vaulted into the van as it reversed out of the driveway. He closed the panel door with a thud. The driver threw the van into gear then accelerated toward her. She only had a lead of a few feet.

She scanned the deserted street. Why wasn't someone out checking their mail or walking their dog?

The van roared closer, its daytime running lights glowing just behind her shoulder. Large cottonwoods with sturdy trunks marched down the strip of grass between the sidewalk and the street. Zoe was sure that if the trees hadn't been there, the van would have jumped the curb to get closer.

The tree trunks flicked by. The van's engine surged and it accelerated in front of her as they approached a cross street. Whispering Wind Court, Zoe thought with relief. She cut diagonally across the yard of the house on the corner and sprinted into the small cul-de-sac.

It was part of her regular route. She normally jogged down the stubby street to add an extra couple of tenths of a mile to her jog, but there had been that day when rain poured down unexpectedly, and she'd used the easement between two houses on the far end of the cul-de-sac as a shortcut to get to her own street.

The van turned onto the cul-de-sac, brakes squealing. Zoe's feet pounded through the thick grass as she made for the opening between the two houses. Leaves brushed her shoulders as she sprinted down the narrow opening between the hedges. She checked her speed slightly. *Hadn't there been a drop off?* The ground dipped away from the homes into a narrow basin then rose again to meet the backyards of the homes on Zoe's street. She stepped cautiously over a stack of tree limbs near piles of grass clippings. This was the dumping ground for the yard waste from the homes on the cul-de-sac. With the sudden slow down, her labored breathing sounded loud.

Brakes screeched and the solid whoosh of the van's panel door sliding open carried across the quiet neighborhood. She high-stepped through the grass clippings, found the drop off of about three feet and skittered down, bringing a shower of dry grass and leaves with her. A few steps through some squishy, damp ground at the low point, and then she scrambled up the far side through more leaves and loose branches. She couldn't help taking a quick look over her shoulder.

The stocky man burst out from between the hedges, spotted her on the other side of the depression, and hesitated. Zoe could see that he was torn between following her and going back to the van. Zoe didn't wait to see what he decided. She dove into the dim corridor between two houses, crossed the lawn, and hit the sidewalk at a run, automatically turning in the direction of her house.

It was only three houses away, and her feet flew across the short distance. She cut across her yard and sprinted up the driveway, then jerked to a stop.

Did they know where she lived? They obviously knew where she jogged. Breathing hard, she looked longingly at her house. She wanted to run inside and deadbolt the door, but if they were coming here, that was the last place she should go.

Zoe switched direction, sprinted to her neighbor's house, and reached over the gate to unlatch it from the inside. She walked Torrie's dog a few times a week, but this week Torrie was visiting family, and she'd taken her labrador with her. Zoe was as familiar with Torrie's house as she was with her own. Zoe went to the brick patio, pried up the third brick from the left and removed the house key from its hiding place. The rough brick slipped from her trembling fingers and fell back into place.

She shoved it into alignment and raced up the steps to the kitchen door. She got the door unlocked with only a little fumbling then punched in the code to disable the alarm.

Zoe closed the kitchen door and leaned against it for a second, listening for the sound of the van in her driveway next door. The wind rattled a window screen. The solid tick of the grandfather clock in the living room measured the silence. She ran a shaky hand over her mouth. Her fingers smelled of dust from the brick. She sucked in a deep breath then blew it out, trying to calm her racing heartbeat as she went to peek out the living room window to the street.

The white van cruised by in one direction, moving slowly. The driver, Mr. Unibrow, swiveled his head from side to side. Zoe swallowed and watched the van reach the end of the street, make a three-point-turn, then retrace its route. It didn't slowdown at her house, but continued at a slow pace until it reached the other end of the street. It sat there for a moment, red brake lights glowing, and then it made a hard right and accelerated away.

Zoe let out a whoosh of breath, but didn't move from the window. She stayed there a full fifteen minutes. She knew that much time had gone by because the grandfather clock chimed the quarter hour twice, each time nearly giving her a heart attack. She decided that they really weren't coming back.

Zoe locked up Torrie's house then scurried over to her house. The first thing she did was check every door and window. Had the attempt to get her been a random thing? Had Mr. Unibrow and his stocky companion gone after her simply because she was a lone female in a deserted neighborhood? She came slowly down the stairs, running over the whole incident again.

No, she didn't think it had been a coincidence. There had been something about the way Mr. Unibrow studied her as he slowed the van to her pace. He had thoroughly checked her face before he blocked her path. She shivered, despite still having a sheen of sweat on her after her frantic race home.

And, there had been two of them, a team. Not some loner weirdo, attacking women in a deserted area, like she heard about on the news. She paused on the last step, her hand tight on the banister. No, it had been coordinated, and it was only because she knew the neighborhood better than they did that she was here at home and not in the back of that van.

Faintly, she heard a car move down the street. Her heart rate, which had settled into a normal rhythm, jumped back to high gear. She moved stealthily toward the living room window. The tension drained out of her as she watched a familiar SUV cruise by. Zoe recognized the driver, a mom who lived down the street and seemed to spend half her day in the SUV, shuttling her kids to and from school and activities.

Zoe spun away from the window, suddenly angry that the sound of a car moving down her street made her afraid. She stalked into the kitchen, snatched up the phone, and found the card the FBI agents had left. But instead of dialing, she switched the phone from hand to hand. She didn't have much to tell them, no specifics—just a white van and general descriptions about the two guys. She didn't have a license plate number or even a witness. Sato in particular was already doubtful about the silver car. What would he say when she called with the news that another vehicle had not only followed her, but a passenger had come after her?

No, she wasn't going to open herself up to more questions. Donna hadn't been big on life lessons or making good choices, but one thing Zoe had absorbed from growing up with Donna was not to trust anyone. She'd trusted Jack and look where that had landed her. No, better to stay wary of everyone, including the FBI. It didn't matter that Mort had seemed to believe her about the money. Sato hadn't. And, he'd doubted her story about the silver car. The last thing she wanted to do was come off as a crazy conspiracy theory nut.

Another car hummed down the street and she tensed, leaning sideways to check the small section of the street she could see out the window over the sink. A small red Accord motored by and she relaxed.

The file folder was still open on the kitchen island. Maybe the skull and crossbones sketch hadn't been meant to indicate that Jack was in trouble. Maybe it had been meant for her, a warning.

She replaced the phone and bit her lip as an idea took shape. Staying here was out of the question. It wasn't safe. Even if the guys in the white van didn't know exactly where her house was, a few days parked on the street in a different car, and they'd be able to find her. Whoever had been in the silver car definitely knew her address. Were they working together?

She ran her hands over her hair, pushing a few strands, which had come loose, off her forehead. She didn't have time to worry about the possible variables of the silver car and the van. She needed to get out of here, get somewhere safe. Her first thought was Helen's house, but she didn't want to put her in danger so that was out.

A second, crazier, idea came to her as she stared at the file folder, which was still open on the island. She needed to get out of town and go someplace where no one would find her —or even think of looking for her. If she needed to leave town anyway, why not go to the place that kept popping up? Why not London?

She went to her laptop. First, she pulled up her bank account and checked her savings balance, which made her cringe—her usual reaction—then she did a search for airline tickets to London.

While she waited for the page to load, she reread the article on cyber crime that mentioned the leading expert, Dave Bent, who was based in London. Maybe she should hire this Bent guy to help her find the money. Not that she had any money to pay him with, but if it came down to her word against the FBI, she would need someone on her side, and as much as she knew Helen's lawyer husband would help her out, he wasn't a criminal lawyer. Wouldn't it be better to have a computer expert searching for the money?

The airline webpage loaded, and she bit her lip when she saw the price. Even off-season, a roundtrip ticket would wipe out her savings. But what choice did she have? Hide out here and wait for the next person to follow her? Confide in the FBI and hope they believed her and could protect her? But how could they protect her when she wasn't even sure what she needed protection from?

She took a deep breath and hit the PURCHASE button. She'd never been the type of person to agonize over decisions. She figured now wasn't the time to start.

She had credit cards—thank goodness she'd managed to pay the balances down—and she'd rather be proactive than reactive. She'd had enough of waiting around. It was time for action.

She printed her boarding pass and went off to shower and change into fresh clothes, feeling better and more in control.

She operated better on the fly and, if nothing else, a trip to London would confuse everyone. At least she had a plan: go to London, look up the cyber crimes guy, see if he could find out what was going on with the missing money, and figure out what the Covent Garden web link meant.

Okay, it barely qualified as a plan and details were so sketchy that they were almost non-existent, but she was spontaneous and did her best thinking on her feet. She threw some clothes in a suitcase, found her passport, and sent Helen a text, asking her to come by on her way home from work.

When Helen arrived two hours later, Zoe was shutting down her laptop. "What's this?" Helen asked, noticing the suitcase parked at the door.

"I need a ride to the airport."

"The airport?" Helen sounded as if Zoe had asked for a ride to Mars.

"Yes. I'm going to visit my mom."

"What about Thanksgiving? I thought you were spending it with us? And, you never go visit your mom..." Helen's voice trailed off as she noticed the open file on the island.

Zoe reached to close it, but Helen was faster and pounced. "These are articles about Italy and about Jack," she said as she rifled through the papers. She looked up, her head tilted to one side and her eyes narrowed. "You're not going to visit your mom. Something is going on, isn't it? Something related to Jack?"

Zoe seized the file from Helen's hands and quickly slipped it into the messenger bag along with her laptop. "I'm *telling* you I'm going to visit my mom."

The corners of Helen's mouth turned down and she put

her hands on her hips. "Oh, I see. You're telling me where you're not going, so that I'll be able to pass this misinformation on to the FBI when they come to visit me. No way. Not again."

"It's better this way," Zoe said and hurried on before Helen could protest again. "I hate not telling you everything, but it's safer. Something is wrong—very wrong—and I'm not going to have you pulled into it, too. It's bad enough what happened to me today. I'm not going to tell you what it was, except to say that it involved running for my life."

Helen had been drawing a breath to continue her argument, but she paused and her expression turned from bullish to concerned. "Running for your life?"

Zoe touched Helen's arm as she said, "Don't look so worried. I'm not sticking around to give them a second chance. That's why I'm leaving."

"What—"

Zoe held up her hand. "I'm sorry, but I'm not telling you anything else. I wish I could, but I don't want you to get mixed up in this, too."

Helen's face reflected her internal debate. Finally, she sighed. "Okay. I won't waste my breath. I know that stubborn expression. You've made up your mind, and there's nothing I can do to change it. Just like when you were determined to toilet paper Mike Halliday's house in ninth grade."

A smile crept onto Zoe's face at the memory. "How was I supposed to know their invisible dog fence included the front yard?" Zoe and Helen had had one tree festooned with toilet paper streamers when the Hallidays' let their dogs out. Surrounded by barking and growling dogs, they'd done the only thing they could to get out of the reach of those sharp white canine teeth. They'd scrambled up the tree—the one they'd just decorated with toilet paper. Mr. Halliday along with Mike and his younger sister found them when they came to investigate what all the yapping was about. It wasn't the most mortifying experience of Zoe's life, but it was definitely in the top five.

"How are you even paying for this?" Helen asked, dropping onto one of the barstools. A last minute ticket to..., well, anywhere, even someplace close like Houston is outrageous."

"I have some money saved. The ceiling will have to wait a little longer is all," Zoe said. Helen was about to say something else, but Zoe moved to the door. "Are you taking me to the airport or not? Because I can drive myself, but then I'll have to pay long-term parking, and you know how outrageously expensive that is."

"Okay, okay. Let's go," Helen said as she stood and threw her purse strap on her shoulder. "It's a good thing we're best friends, you know that, right?"

"Wouldn't have it any other way," Zoe said as she wheeled her suitcase out of the kitchen and locked the door.

"Is it done?" Anna asked, keeping her voice low. The stone floors and walls of the enormous hallway echoed despite the thick carpets and the heavy tapestries on the walls.

She could barely hear Wade's voice on the bad connection of the cell phone line as he said, "No."

"No?" Her voice reverberated on the cold stone. Forcing herself to speak softly, she bit off each word. "What happened?"

"She got away. Ran through the neighborhood, took a shortcut that we didn't know was there. Just disappeared."

"We? *We*?" she repeated. "You brought someone else in on this?"

"I had to. Couldn't do it by myself."

"You idiot." Anna forced herself not to say anything else. She wouldn't be able to speak without yelling, and she couldn't draw any attention to herself. She closed her eyes and fought down the mist of anger. As she calmed down, she became aware that he was still speaking.

"...two person job. That way, there was one to grab her and one to drive. Quicker." After a few seconds, the words, "You still there, Anna?" came through the phone.

"No names," she hissed. "I told you that."

"Sorry," he mumbled.

She cut across the word. "Who did you involve?"

"It's fine. He's a buddy of mine from high school. I didn't tell him anything. He doesn't even know you're involved."

"Really? He just agreed to help you snatch a woman off the street while she was jogging?"

"Well, sure. I told him I had a thing for redheads."

"That's all it took? A few words and he agreed to help you commit a felony?"

The silence stretched. "And I told him I'd pay him ten."

"You do realize you're vulnerable now, don't you?"

"Vulnerable? To what?"

She rubbed the bridge of her nose. "To blackmail."

"What?"

"Never mind. The ten thousand comes out of your cut, and he's your problem. I suggest you make it clear there will be no more money after that."

"Ah, sure. I can do that."

"You'd better."

"Why didn't you go to her house—you and your *buddy*? You could have taken care of it there."

"Ah, well. That's why I was calling. What was that address again? I *memorized* it like you said, but...even you have to admit that it was kind of confusing. It had so many fives. Was it five-two-five-one? Or five-two-one-five?"

Anna closed her eyes and breathed out through her nose before replying. "Five-two-five-one."

"Wow. You didn't even have to look it up."

"No. You know why? Because I memorized it."

"Hey, I can't help it if I've got dyslexia."

"Just get it over with." Anna paced down the hall a few steps to a window and studied the dusting of snow on the trees and grass, a study in monochrome tones.

"Ah...right. Sure. No probs."

"Call me when you have her."

8

While she waited for her flight out of DFW, Zoe had a few terrible moments of misgiving. She almost expected to see Sato sprinting down the concourse to prevent her from catching the flight. She forcibly pushed that image aside and reminded herself that she had done nothing wrong. There was no reason she couldn't take a little trip. No one had specifically told her not to leave town.

A little voice whispered in her ear, "Yeah, but it sure was implied."

She chose to ignore that voice. She wasn't going home to wait meekly for someone to tail her again or attempt to pull her off the street into a strange van. No, action was better.

And it was the week of Thanksgiving. It would probably be days before anyone at the FBI even figured out she wasn't in Dallas. Hopefully, it would be at least a week before Mort heard about the silver car—government bureaucracy and all that. She made a mental note to check her emails and voice messages faithfully and to reply to any contact from Mort or Sato right away. No need to give them any reason to seek her out, especially at her now empty home.

Her boarding group was called and she wedged herself into her seat in coach, feeling like an anonymous human sardine.

She felt more relaxed at Newark, where she had to change planes. If the FBI wanted to prevent her from leaving the country, she felt sure that would have happened in Dallas. While she waited at the gate, she used the airport Wi-Fi to rough out her next step. She looked up two hotels listed in the *Smart Travel* London guidebook that she'd grabbed off her shelf at the last moment when Helen wasn't watching. She emailed the first one, a boutique hotel near Victoria Station, and received a reply that they did have a room available and would be happy to hold it for her. She made a mental note to let the *Smart Travel* editor she worked with know the guidebook lived up to its name.

Next, she re-read the article about cyber crime and did an Internet search for the expert, Dave Bent. It wasn't hard to find him. He had a website. As a consultant, he specialized in corporate cyber security and had provided expertise to various organizations, including Interpol, MI-5, and the FBI.

She tried not to think about the international charges as she dialed Dave Bent's office number. A clipped female voice requested she leave a message. Zoe kept it short, giving only her first name and phone number. With the time difference, he was probably already gone for the day and the office was closed. Zoe mapped the office location and consulted her guidebook. It was near the Leicester Square tube, only a few stops away from her hotel. If she didn't have a message from

Mr. Bent by the time she landed, she'd simply drop by his office.

"Passenger Hunter, please see me at the podium." The gate agent replaced the microphone after the announcement.

Zoe didn't move from her chair in the back corner of the waiting area near the gate. She scanned the crowd, her pulse thumping, but didn't see any FBI-types.

The next announcement was for pre-boarding, and passengers jumped up from their chairs, jockeying to get as close to the gate as they could before their boarding group was called. She remained where she was until she was sure neither Mort, Sato, or anyone else who looked remotely like they might be an official of the US government were lurking in the crowd. The gate agent repeated the announcement about passenger Hunter, and Zoe reluctantly moved to the podium.

The woman asked to see her boarding pass, and Zoe slid it across the counter. The woman switched it for another one. "You've been upgraded." She smiled. "First class. You can board at any time through our special access lane."

"There must be a mistake. I didn't pay for first class," Zoe said, already mentally kicking herself. Who turned down first class?

"It seems another passenger recognized you and wanted to surprise you." She tilted her head toward a man who stood partially hidden behind the tall wall dividers that displayed the gate number and flight information. "But if you'd rather not take the new seat, I can switch you back..."

Zoe instantly recognized the silver hair, the dark stubble, and the warm brown eyes. "Sam?" Zoe stepped away from the counter. "What are you doing here?" Instead of his usual casual T-shirt and shorts or oxford shirt and khakis, he wore a yellow tie, white dress shirt, black dress pants, and had a suit jacket over his arm.

"Flying to London, just like you. I figured we should sit together."

"In first class?" Sam was a struggling businessman. How could he afford first class for one person, much less two? And, he was in a suit? Up until that moment, Zoe would have bet money that he didn't even *own* a suit.

The gate agent watched them, her eyebrows raised. Zoe hesitated.

"Please sit with me," Sam said, extending his arm toward the jet way. He still wore the woven leather bands on his wrist along with his expensive watch. Zoe thought his dark eyes looked as pleading as Torrie's labrador. "I'll explain everything on the way, I promise."

Zoe took the new boarding pass.

The special trappings of the first class cabin took all the time before departure. There were a surprising amount of issues to be sorted out. Would Mr. Clark like his suit jacket hung up? Would Ms. Hunter prefer a drink before takeoff? Which main course did Ms. Hunter prefer, roast lamb with mushrooms, spinach pasta, or grilled chicken with asparagus?

Then there was all the stuff that came with the special seat assignment. Zoe juggled the thick blanket, pillow, headphones, and the zippered amenity kit, which contained a sleep mask, mints, toothbrush and toothpaste, a comb, and lotion. There was so much legroom that she couldn't reach the seatback pocket in front of her without doing stretches that belonged in a yoga class, so she stuffed the freebies down the side of her oversized recliner-like seat that had more bells and whistles than the dashboard on her Jetta.

Surreptitiously, she watched the other passengers, including Sam, as they settled in for the flight. Everyone removed their shoes then most people focused on hooking up various electronic gadgets to charge in the outlets and USB ports built into the seats.

About an hour into the flight, things settled down and Zoe turned to Sam. "Thank you for this." Zoe nodded at her tray, now covered with a linen square and set with a cloth napkin, real silverware, miniature salt and peppershakers, and squares of butter.

"It was the least I could do for you. You've gone out of your way to take care of me at the office."

Zoe nibbled on her snack of mixed warm nuts and sipped a ginger ale. "So, you travel like this often?"

Sam laughed. "Some. Can you tell?"

"You're not agog, like I am. And you know how to work all the controls on the chair as well as the entertainment system." Zoe glanced at the screen he had removed from its hidden compartment and casually flipped into place.

"Fresh bread?" The flight attendant held out a silver breadbasket with a variety of rolls and quick breads.

Zoe chose a slice of Asiago cheese bread, and Sam had a dinner roll. "I haven't been completely honest with you." Sam put his knife on the china plate beside his uneaten roll. "I'm not a struggling small business owner."

Zoe ate a bit of the warm bread and tilted her head. She'd learned from growing up with ever-evasive Donna that she got a lot more information if she kept quiet.

"Encore is a new business—that wasn't a fabrication—but

I already own another successful chain of stores that resells used sports equipment. It's called Rebound. Have you heard of it?"

Zoe choked a bit on the bread, but managed to swallow it. "Oh, yes." She knew there were at least two Rebound stores in her part of Dallas. "I bought some in-line skates there once."

Sam waited a moment, and when she didn't say anything else, he continued, "I've found that it's better for me to work incognito, especially when I'm involved in a new venture. I find out the truth that way—who works hard, who is a slacker, that kind of thing."

"An undercover boss. I can see how that would be helpful."

The flight attendant stopped a rolling cart at their row. "Appetizers? I have skewered shrimp, cheese ravioli, and mango and raspberry salad. Would you like some of each?"

Zoe figured this was a once-in-a-lifetime experience and said, "Sure."

After the cart rolled on, Sam had some of his salad, then said, "I'm sorry I didn't tell you the truth."

"I wish you had, but this is quite a way to apologize," Zoe said as she considered how to eat the shrimp skewers elegantly. Is there a way to eat anything on a skewer elegantly? She gave up on nibbling and popped a whole shrimp in her mouth, which gave her the excuse of not speaking. She wasn't quite sure what to think of Sam. With his puppy-dog eyes and soft-spoken manner it was hard to be upset with him, but he had deceived her and that was something she'd learned not to take lightly.

"So what takes you to London?" he asked.

Zoe dabbed at her lips with her napkin. "Research."

"Oh, the travel books. I didn't realize you wrote them as well. I thought you were the copy-editor."

"*Smart Travel* believes in thorough fact-checking." They did. It had never involved her traveling internationally, but she wasn't about to tell Sam her real reason for going to London. In the first place, it would sound absurd, and, in the second place, if she wasn't going to confide in Helen, she certainly wasn't going to tell anyone else. "What about you? Travel to London often?"

"No, not often. I usually hit more destinations on the continent. France, Italy, Germany."

"Hmm. For some reason, I wouldn't have thought that there would be a big market for used sports equipment in Europe."

"Skis," Sam said. "Used skis are very popular in the winter in all the alpine areas. I'm glad this worked out. These international flights are so long. This one will go faster with you here."

"Yes, traveling first class on international flights is such a drag," Zoe teased, and he shrugged.

"It does get old after a while," he said. "Don't get me wrong. I appreciate all the luxury of first class, but it's still nine hours on an airplane. I've spent my time in coach. All the seats on the plane get there at the same time."

"True," Zoe murmured and sipped her ginger ale. "Funny how it worked out, that we were on the same flight."

"I'm glad I saw you in the waiting area. We could have gone through the whole flight and never known the other person was on the plane."

"Ships passing in the night," Zoe said. "Except we'd be

passengers flying in the same direction, not nearly so roman-
tic-sounding."

"Oh, I don't know about that," he said and she felt a blush
creep into her cheeks as he kept his gaze focused on her
intensely.

Their entrees arrived and they moved on to talk about
other things—the food, what they wanted to see in London.
Zoe didn't need to consult a guidebook to know the hot spots
—Buckingham Palace, St. Paul's Cathedral, the Tower, the
London Eye. Sam said he wanted to see the wax museum, but
wasn't sure if he would have time for sightseeing.

The food kept coming—a selection of cheese and fruit,
then a made-to-order sundae. Zoe felt like she wouldn't need
to eat for another week by the time the linen was cleared.
The cabin lights dimmed, and Zoe tried to settle back with
her mask over her eyes to sleep. She'd never been good at
sleeping on planes and found that having a chair that
reclined to a fully flat position and supported her feet didn't
help her get to dreamland any faster than the seats in coach.
The incidents of the last few days kept cycling through her
mind: the silver car, the unexpected package, the flight from
the white van.

With a huff, she rolled to her side and felt the ring slide
on the chain around her neck.

"Trouble sleeping?" Sam asked.

She pushed up her eye mask and found herself face-to-
face with Sam, who was on his side, mirroring her posture.
He wasn't wearing a sleep mask. She wondered if he'd been
watching her the whole time, or if she'd woken him with her
restlessness.

She shifted backward. "Too much on my mind."

"Ah. Reconsidering?" he asked.

"Reconsidering what?"

"This." He waved a hand back and forth between them. "Perhaps you would rather we stay professional—owner and renter, not friends?" His face was serious, his dark eyes somber.

"I thought we were friends already."

"Yes, but not close friends." He smiled slowly as he emphasized the word "close" and, while the word was innocuous, there was a world of meaning in his tone. Zoe felt her heartbeat speed up, and she suddenly thought about what she must look like. She was sure her hair was going in every direction possible. The sleep mask had probably removed what little make-up she had on. She *had* put on makeup today, hadn't she? And, of course, in her rush to leave, she'd thrown on one of her oldest tops, a faded orange shirt that made her freckles pop.

She smoothed her hair behind her ears. "Close friends, uh? Well, we'd probably need to spend some more time together..."

Sam's face split into a large grin. "Definitely. Lots more time. In fact, we should have dinner together."

"We just had dinner, a very expensive one, actually."

He waved his hand, as if brushing away the upgrade to first class. "A proper dinner. In London."

"That sounds nice."

9

Z oe and Sam paused in the airport after emerging from the plane. He had checked luggage. She didn't. People flowed around them as they both went to speak then both stopped.

Awkward, Zoe thought shifting from foot to foot. "Well... I'm here for a few days."

"Me, too," Sam said as he checked his phone.

Zoe watched him and shook her head slightly. Great. Another guy so connected to his technology that he can't look at me when we talk. That had been one of the issues between her and Jack. It sounds like a trivial thing, but when they were married, she'd often felt as if Jack paid more attention to his phone than to her. Although that wasn't quite fair. He hadn't behaved that way when they traveled together, she remembered.

Sam rattled off a string of familiar numbers, pulling Zoe's attention to the present.

"So, that's right?" he asked. "That's your cell phone?"

"Yes, that's it," Zoe said.

"Great. I'll call you about dinner."

"Sounds good," she said then thought about international calling rates. "Send me a text."

"Okay. Good-bye for now. It was a pleasure." He leaned in, and she realized he was going to kiss her. Now? When she's just spent nine hours on a plane and hadn't been able to brush her teeth because they hit turbulence on the way in, and they all had to stay seated for the last hours of the flight? She did a quick weave move and his lips landed on her cheek. His stubble scratched against her face as his lips brushed her cheek. He smelled of coffee along with a hint of woodsy cologne. She pulled away quickly, blindly grabbed for the handle of her suitcase, and knocked it over.

"Easy there," he said as he set it upright. There was no mistaking the playful smile he sent her. He knew he'd discombobulated her...with a little peck on the cheek. She said good-bye and managed to walk away, thankfully without tripping over her own feet.

Why had she reacted like a schoolgirl? Zoe shook her head at herself as she headed for passport control. She had more serious things to worry about than Sam.

After working her way through the bureaucracy required to enter the country, Zoe found a place to exchange the stack of dollar bills she'd withdrawn on the way to the airport for pounds, then headed for the Underground. She bought a pass, figured out she needed the Blue Line to Piccadilly then she could switch to the Green Line at South Kensington, which would take her to Victoria, the stop closest to her hotel. Zoe levered herself into one of the train cars and found she could hardly keep her eyes open as it swayed down the track. She drifted off, then jerked awake, afraid she'd missed her stop. She hadn't.

Determined to stay awake, she thought over the flight. She never would have thought she'd get to fly first class. It was quite a change from her last transatlantic flight when she and Jack had been in coach. Jack would have loved the lamb —it was one of his favorites and the one time Zoe had tried to cook it for him, she'd burned it. They'd ordered a pizza. She smiled at the memory then suddenly felt disloyal to Sam. Sam was the one who used his points—or miles, whatever— to upgrade her. She should be thinking about Sam, not Jack. The train neared her transfer station, and she forcibly put thoughts of any men—Sam, Jack, even the FBI guys, who always seemed to be hovering ominously at the back of her thoughts—out of her mind and focused on getting to her hotel.

———

HOURS later, Zoe stifled a yawn as she emerged from the Leicester Square tube station. She shouldn't be tired. She had dumped her luggage in her hotel room and ignored all the advice about powering through and forcing yourself to stay awake to get on the new time zone. Instead, she'd collapsed on the bed for a thoroughly satisfying nap. She'd awoken feeling refreshed and was able to fully appreciate the hotel.

It was a small family-run place with ten rooms on a street of immaculate row houses. A short flight of steps rose between white columns to a cobalt blue door. Inside, there were hardwood floors covered in thick cherry-colored rugs and drapes in the same color. Her room was tiny, barely bigger than the double bed, but it had a bath and a tiny wrought-iron enclosed balcony overlooking the narrow back garden. After a shower and fresh clothes, she felt like she could navigate London.

The cool air felt wonderful on her face as she moved away from the tube station. She was glad to be above ground. The long, steep escalator ride from the train platform to the surface had made her feel a bit queasy. It was overcast with the threat of drizzle hanging in the dark clouds as she made her way through the souvenir and T-shirt shops, consulting the map that came with the *Smart Travel* guidebook. She dug her chin in to the lime-colored scarf she had wrapped around her neck, glad she'd worn Helen's hand-me-down boots.

She would have liked to explore the small park in the square surrounded by shops and restaurants, but Dave Bent's office was in the other direction. As she walked, she couldn't help but compare London to her other international travel experience, Italy. There were the same narrow streets, some of them with cobblestones, but London didn't have the air of unruliness and disorder that reigned in Naples.

The London streets were neat and clean, at least in this part of the city. There was no graffiti, no trash. The buildings were mostly brick in this area and only a few stories high, so she didn't get that closed in, canyon-like feeling that there had been in Naples. There was no crumbling stucco or peeling advertisement posters on these meticulously maintained buildings. The paint on the doors and on the trim around the buildings was sharp and fresh. Cars seemed to stay in their lanes, for the most part, or were slotted into the carefully marked spaces along the street. It all looked so orderly and tidy.

She passed the iconic red phone box and smiled. She was in London. She savored the thought for a moment, then whipped out her phone and snapped a picture of the phone box as well as some of the shops, which were decorated for Christmas with lights, bows, and plenty of fake snow. She captured photos of the street, the shops, and the architecture as she walked. Reluctantly, she put her phone away, checked her map again, and realized that when the road split a few streets back, she'd picked the wrong angle and was actually moving diagonally, farther away from Dave Bent's office.

She made a quick right to get on the correct street and thought she saw someone who looked like Sam darting across the street after her. She spun fully around and searched the pedestrians moving along the sidewalk. Could it have been him? Had his business brought him to Leicester Square as well? The crowds shifted.

No, she was wrong. She navigated the streets until she found number twenty-seven on a short street with a mix of commercial shops and a few restaurants.

She pushed through the double doors of dark wood that framed glass panels. She stopped in the small marble-tiled entryway with three doors, all closed, a steep wooden stairway, and a narrow elevator. She moved to the door with the discreet gold lettering that read, BENT CONSULTING, unsure if she should knock. She settled for a quick tap and then opened the door without waiting.

The building looked as if it had been a home before it had been converted to offices. This room must have been a closet. One step brought her inside the room and to the edge of the receptionist's desk where a young woman was hastily hiding her cell phone in a drawer.

"Yes?" She pushed her long golden blond hair behind her shoulders, picked up a pen, and tapped a pad of paper on her cluttered desk as if Zoe had interrupted some important task.

"I'd like to see Dave Bent." The walls of the tiny reception area were filled with framed news articles that mentioned him. One article, positioned on the wall behind the receptionist, showed a slightly pudgy man in his twenties with a goatee and thick brown hair drooping down over his forehead to the edges of his circular glasses.

"He's not in. Did you have an appointment?"

Zoe could see through the doorway behind the receptionist into a tiny space that looked more like an overflowing storage container rather than an office. Zoe could just make out the edge of a desk under a mountain of papers, books, and magazines, along with several computers. Books, notebooks, papers, and odd miscellanea filled bookshelves that lined the walls. Tables crowded with computers were wedged up against the bookcases, and power cords and cables snaked across the floor. Sticky notes covered everything: the computers, the desk, the spines of books, even the windows.

As she watched, one of the sticky notes detached and drifted to a pile of papers and books mounded in a chair in front of the desk. Zoe half expected the bit of paper to cause a cascade, but the paper merely glanced off the pile, then floated to the floor where it joined several other notes. It was like some sort of strange paper manifestation of the geological process. She tore her gaze away from the disorder. "No. I only need a few minutes of his time. When will he be in?"

She shrugged.

"Okay. I'll leave a message," Zoe said, and the receptionist grudgingly wrote down the number. He's never going to get that message, Zoe thought. Impulsively, she added, "I'd like to interview him for an article I'm writing about cyber crime and Victor Costa."

The receptionist sighed. "Who do you work for?"

"*The Informationalist,*" she said, naming the blog that had broken so much news about Jack's story.

"Never heard of it," she said suspiciously, but wrote it down on the slip of paper. This Bent guy seemed to like to do interviews.

"We're on-line only. American." She didn't look convinced, so Zoe added, "My name is Jenny Singletarry." If Jenny ever found out she'd used her name, there would be no more slipping out of interview requests, but if Zoe could just get the guy to call her, she might be able to convince him to look into the bank transfers. Surely he'd be curious. And, this way, if Dave Bent looked up the website, he would find plenty of articles with that byline. "It's really important he call me at that number," Zoe said, thinking that if he contacted *The Informationalist* directly through their website contact page, she would be blown. "It's the only number where he can reach me while I'm in London." The receptionist had put down her pen, so Zoe added, "You need to put that on the note—this number only."

The receptionist rolled her eyes, but added the information.

"Thank you." Zoe turned to leave as the receptionist tore the paper off the pad and moved to take it into the messy office.

"You'll make sure he gets the message?" Zoe asked doubtfully, watching as the woman tossed it on the heap on the desk.

"It may look like chaos," she said returning to her chair, "but he's got a system." She'd returned to texting before Zoe closed the door.

ZOE strolled through the shops of Covent Garden. Pale green steel beams stretched to the glass ceiling that covered the two-level open air arcaded shopping area. She stopped and admired a shell-shaped dish painted with blue flowers at one of the stores, then returned it to the table when she thought of her credit card balance, which had taken quite a hit this morning when she checked into the hotel. No impulse purchases for her. The whole trip was an impulse purchase, she reminded herself and moved on. The neighborhood around Covent Garden was also known by the same name, but since the GPS coordinates had centered on the complex that had once been the flower, fruit, and vegetable market, she'd walked directly here from Dave Bent's office. Since she'd missed the computer expert, she hoped she'd have better luck here.

She maneuvered around a Christmas tree and continued her stroll. Fairy lights, mistletoe, Santas, and red bows abounded. She paused to check out a display of wooden toys, then continued her walk. The shopping area was huge, and she didn't even know what she was looking for. She sighed, feeling overwhelmed.

Despite her nap, her arms and legs felt heavy. Sleepiness crept up on her again. She had no idea what Jack had been trying to tell her. Her mood was as gloomy as the gray clouds pressing down on the glass roof.

Had she just blown her savings and risked annoying the FBI by skipping the country on a whim? She supposed she could change the date on her return ticket, which was set for six days from now. Could she get back to Dallas before Mort and Sato realized she had left?

Food. That was what she needed, she decided. She hadn't thought she'd be hungry after the food served in first class—there had been a midnight snack of warm cookies and a light breakfast shortly before they landed—but it was after three and she hadn't had lunch. There was a pub-like place across the arcade and she headed down the steps toward it, but once she was on the lower level, her steps faltered, and she stopped in front of a pizzeria.

"Bella Napoli," she whispered, reading the name and moved to the door of the restaurant. She'd spent two days in Napoli, the Italian name for Naples, with Jack. A mural dominated one wall, depicting the curving sweep of the Bay of Naples. A mishmash of buildings filled the plain that sloped down to the sea, crowding against the water's edge while the dark shadow of Mt. Vesuvius loomed in the background.

"Sit anywhere you like," said a passing waiter, and Zoe took a table at the rear near the dark triangle of Mt. Vesuvius. She ordered a margarita pizza from a blonde coed and watched the other diners as the servers moved between the tables and the kitchen, which contained a large wood-fired pizza oven. Her pizza came and it was an authentic Neapolitan pizza with buffalo mozzarella, a few sprigs of basil dotting the tomato sauce, and a crust that was thin, but not too crispy.

She savored every bite of the pizza. She ordered a black coffee and sipped it as she paid the bill, then lingered, searching every aspect of the restaurant. The caffeine gave her a jolt of energy, and she scrutinized the faces of the servers moving through the tables, the other customers, and the mosaic on the wall. She even reexamined the menu, then shoved it into the holder on the table in frustration. Just because the restaurant was called Napoli didn't mean it was connected to Jack. She was probably completely wrong about the numbers and was on a wild goose chase. She threw her napkin on the table and shoved her chair back.

"Signorina, I am so sorry that you were not pleased with your meal."

"There was nothing wr—" She broke off as she looked up at the young man standing beside her. "Nico," she whispered. She had only met him once when she was in Italy with Jack but he wasn't someone you forgot. He had a charming smile that he had turned up to full blast at the moment. He still had the same short black hair combed up into a spike that ran down the center of his head. Instead of the trendy skinny jeans and tight shirt that he'd worn when she met him, he now wore an apron with dusty flour marks on it over chef's pants and a loose white T-shirt.

Nico spoke over her, drowning out her words. "Please, it is no problem." He took her hand and pressed a paper into it. "Take these coupons, and please accept my deepest apologies."

She frowned at him, but his expression kept her from saying anything. His smile never wavered, but there was caution in his eyes, and he shook his head slightly, a tiny movement, but Zoe picked up on it. He clutched her hand in a tight clasp. When she'd met him the other time, he'd taken her hand and deposited a kiss on it in a playful way. He'd been a bit of clown then, but there was nothing playful about the way he gripped her hand now.

He squeezed her hand, and she squeezed back. "Yes, um, thank you." Nico released her hand and stepped away as she rose from her seat. He returned to the kitchen. She left the restaurant without looking over her shoulder.

She made herself walk a full thirty paces and stopped to browse in two stores before she pulled the coupons out of her pocket. On the back of one was scribbled, "Pig and Rose in twenty minutes."

10

"The Pig and Rose?" Zoe muttered. That had to be a pub, but how was she going to find it? She couldn't afford a smart phone and couldn't look the name up online. Her very basic phone's only advanced feature was the now rather anti-quated ability to flip open. She scrambled to the index of her guidebook and found a listing for the pub along with an address. *Smart Travel* was right—their guidebooks really were the best. She asked a shop clerk for directions and walked through the carnival atmosphere of the streets around Covent Garden. She dodged a mime, navigated around a magician, and a man painted head-to-toe in copper, who sat motionless on a box in the pose of *The Thinker* while tourists took pictures.

After two wrong turns, she found the pub and slipped inside. It was dim and packed with tourists. As her eyes adjusted, she spotted Nico at a table along the wall. He had changed out of his apron and chef's pants into a sweater and a pair of dark jeans. She moved slowly to join him in case he waved her off since he clearly hadn't wanted anyone to know she knew him at the restaurant. But this time he smiled as he stood and kissed each side of her face, lingering a bit longer than was strictly necessary as he whispered, "You look as beautiful as you did that day in Pompeii."

She pulled away. "Good to see you haven't lost your ability to flirt." His grin widened, and he pulled out a chair for her as she said, "You were so serious back there—you had me worried."

His smile faded. "It is serious. Why did you not come sooner?"

Zoe had been unwinding the scarf from her neck. She stopped. "You were expecting me?"

"Yes. Jack sent you a message this summer. He said you would understand and come."

She draped the scarf over the back of her chair along with her coat. "Then he should have chosen a more reliable messenger," Zoe said, exasperation at her mom lacing her tone. "I didn't get the message until this week."

Nico threw his hands up and let out a stream of Italian. A few heads turned their way, and he immediately quieted down. He shook his head. "No matter. You are here now." Nico tapped the screen on his phone a few times, then showed her a picture of a dark sky lit with a forked stroke of lightning. "Now he will know you are here. Tomorrow, go to this website, Pinterest. Look up "Brianna Smith," and see what has been posted to this board, 'Favorites.' He will send you a message."

"Wait. What are you talking about? The jet lag must have caught up with me because I thought you said something about Pinterest."

"Yes, that is correct. We use it to communicate." Nico tapped the screen. "It is too dangerous for us to call one another or send emails. The pictures are codes," he said slowly as if explaining something to a child.

Zoe shook her head. She'd heard about groups using message boards and websites to communicate, but Pinterest? "Okay. I guess that would be the last place someone would expect Jack to post a message. I'm lightning, you said?"

"Yes, Jack said it was...how do you say? Just right? Appro..."

"Appropriate?"

"Yes." He repeated the word with a suggestive little lift of his eyebrows.

"Stop that. I'm too old for you," she said.

"Age does not matter in affairs of the heart. All is permitted in love and war."

"Still working on your idioms, I see." She took the phone from him and scrolled through the other pictures. There were some of trees, clouds, a high-speed train, another of a movie poster. "So each one of these means something specific?" Nico nodded. "And how will I understand what Jack posts? What's the code?"

The corners of his mouth turned down as he shrugged. "Jack said you will understand it."

Zoe rubbed her head and muttered. "More codes."

"What?"

"Never mind." Zoe pushed her hair behind her ears and sat up straight. "Okay. Tell me about Jack. Where is he?" Nico shrugged. "You don't know? Well, what has he been doing for the last six months?" Another shrug. "Oh, come on. You expect me to believe that Jack sent me this elaborate, risky, and vague message that leads me to you, who I actually manage to stumble into, and the only thing you know is a pin board website?"

Heads swiveled their way again as Zoe finished in a screechy tone. Nico put his hand on her hers, but there was no flirting this time.

Zoe's eyes narrowed. "Have you actually seen him?"

"Yes. Briefly." Nico's face was serious. "He came to Naples, to ask for my help."

"But why would he do that?" Zoe could understand Jack's reluctance to return to the US, where the fraud surrounding GRS was still under investigation, but why would he go to Nico for help?

"I do not know the details. All I know is that he wanted me to get your ring so he could send it to you. He said you would understand it was from him."

"How did you get it? I figured it was lost at the bottom of the canal."

"No, it was with the other evidence in Venice. I asked a friend for a favor and," Nico spread his hands, "now there is no evidence that the polizia ever had it."

Zoe shook her head. "How can that happen? I mean, you can't just go in and remove evidence from the police." Nico's face was bland and unconcerned. "Can you?"

"They should not have kept it. It should have been returned to you. There was no need for them to keep a wedding ring. You are upset that I took it."

"Yes. I'm in enough trouble already." She felt the weight of the ring on its long chain under her shirt shift against her chest as she moved. "I don't need to add stealing evidence to my list of possible illegal activities."

"No one will ever look for that ring. It is fixed. It was not among the things found in the canal. You Americans worry about such small things."

"You're laughing at me," Zoe said, amazed.

"Yes. It is not something you should worry about."

Zoe stared at him a moment, then said, "Okay. Fine. You paid off someone to steal it and fix the records. I hope they keep their mouth shut."

"They will. I paid them well. Besides, they do not want to get on the wrong side of my family."

"All right," Zoe said and realized she was fingering the chain. She snatched her hand away. "Then, let's get back to Jack. Why did he disappear?"

"That is for him to tell you, not me."

That statement made Zoe pause. Nico seemed to know inside information. Jack said it was the reason he had recruited Nico back in Naples. "So you know what happened, and you're not going to tell me?"

He concentrated on the table as he spoke. "Many things in Italy are not as they appear. There are...how do you say... movements under the water?"

"Undercurrents?"

"Yes. That is the word. Sometimes unseen forces move things."

"Who? Who would do that? Everyone involved in the incident is accounted for..." Zoe's voice trailed off. All the players that we knew of, she silently amended. Maybe Costa *had* been involved?

Nico picked up his phone from the table and became very focused on it as he murmured, "It is hard to know who has that influence."

"Nico," Zoe said in a voice she used when she found Torrie's labrador noshing on tissues out of the trashcan. "Was it Costa? Was he involved?"

"I cannot say anything else." His tone was firm. The subject was closed.

Zoe threw herself back in her chair. "So many secrets."

He ignored her words, asking instead, "What would you like to drink?"

"A coffee. Black." She was already jittery. A little more caffeine couldn't hurt.

Nico returned a few minutes later from the bar, carrying an American coffee for her and a beer for himself. They sat in silence for a moment, sipping their drinks then Zoe said, "So why are you here in London?"

"My family has owned the restaurant for ten years." He motioned with his chin in the direction of Covent Garden. "My uncle got sick and the family sent me to help him."

"I see. How long have you been here?"

"Five months."

"Interesting timing."

He didn't say anything, just smiled and sipped his beer.

Zoe watched him over the rim of her cup. "Fine. Don't tell me anything. I'll figure it all out on my own. I'm very good at that."

"That is what Jack says about you."

Zoe looked at him sharply. "Jack said that?" Jack wasn't exactly free with his compliments.

"Yes. He also says you are a pain in—" A person moving through the tables, jostled Nico's chair and he broke off.

"No need to finish." She set her cup down with a click.

"So, you're here in London, helping in the restaurant..." she let her voice trail off and raised her eyebrows.

Nico arranged his face into an expression as innocent as a cupid in an Italian fresco. "What are you asking?"

"Well, surely you have other concerns? You're not here to just make pizza, are you?"

He pulled away, placing a hand on his chest. "*Just* to make pizza? You slander the heritage of my homeland."

"Okay, okay. You're carrying on the fine tradition of authentic Neapolitan pizza making and...what else? I'm sure there are some undercurrents in your family business, too."

He sent her a quick smile. "We would not be Italian, if we did not have other interests besides pizza. We've diversified."

"I bet you have," Zoe muttered into her cup. Nico pretended not to hear her. She swiveled toward him as she had a thought. "Would any of these interests involve computers or software? Technology?"

He shook his head. "No, we are not much in that line. Our focus is more on ...solid items. Why?"

"I need to talk to someone who knows about tracing bank transfers. I thought I had found someone here in London, but that may not work out."

"What's his name?"

"Dave Bent. He's a consultant who works with the police. This whole thing that's blowing up again around Jack involves some money that was transferred out of his business account. If I can get someone to help me figure out where the money went, then I might be able to convince the police that I didn't move it to some secret off-shore account."

Nico leaned back. "Oh, that is easy. You don't need

someone who works with the police. You need someone who knows the illegal side. You need Ares."

"Ares?"

"A code name." Nico pulled a pen from his pocket and wrote on a napkin then handed it to her. "You can contact him through this email."

"He can do that, track bank transfers?"

"Yes," he said, swelling up a bit at the doubt in her tone. "Remember, it is what I do best, knowing things."

She put the napkin in her messenger bag. "How much does he charge?"

"Does it matter?"

"Right. Maybe there's a reward for that money," she said on a sigh. "That's probably the only way I'll be able to pay him."

"Perhaps he will give you a discount."

"Because I know you?" Zoe asked.

"No. Because you are a beautiful woman."

Zoe rolled her eyes and settled her messenger bag on her shoulder as she stood. "In that case, I'll be sure to ask for the pretty woman discount."

"I'M heading out."

Mort looked up from his keyboard. Sato shrugged into his suit jacket and pulled his keys from his pocket. "You staying much later?"

"No. Just finished these notes. Why?"

"You know, day before Thanksgiving. Lots of people heading out early."

Mort glanced around the office and realized it was quieter than usual. Most of the desks were empty, and the background buzz of conversation and ringing phones was missing.

"What are you doing tomorrow?" Sato asked.

Mort removed his half glasses and looked fully at Sato. "We're having friends over. Turkey, dressing, whole nine yards. You want to come over?"

"God, no. I have tickets to the game," he said, referring to the Cowboys' Thanksgiving Day football game. "Just making sure you weren't getting a turkey sandwich at Subway."

Mort gave him a sharp glance. He didn't think anyone knew about that awful first holiday season after his daughter died. Those had been dark days. His wife Kathy had pulled out of the darkness first, little by little, seeming to find solace in working with the cancer society. It had taken Mort much longer to return to some sort of skewed reality.

"Wait. Where's that note?" Mort patted the stack of files then pawed through the papers on his desk. "Kathy wants me to pick up something on the way home..." He checked the floor.

Sato pulled a sticky note off the monitor. "Sage?"

"Yeah. Sage." Mort took the note and slipped it into his breast pocket along with his glasses.

Sato slapped Mort on the shoulder as he turned for the door. "Happy Thanksgiving."

"Happy Thanksgiving," Mort replied as he stood. He put one arm into his suit jacket and hit the refresh button on his email before he threaded his other arm through the sleeve. Nothing else on the silver car that Zoe had seen. He had put out some inquiries, but nothing had popped up.

The CCTV footage from the airport had been a bust as well.

He put the files away then pulled up the address for Martha Baumkirchner in Farmers Branch. It wasn't on the way home, but he was sure he could find a store near her house that sold sage.

IT was late afternoon, but darkness was already descending as Zoe left the pub. The temperature had dropped, and the air was heavy with the scent of ozone. She was glad she had an umbrella tucked into her messenger bag. It looked like she would need it before she got back to the hotel. She could feel her hair expanding exponentially as it absorbed the moisture in the air. Zoe was a block away from the pub when she realized she didn't have her scarf. She did an abrupt about-face and a tall man, with salt and pepper hair, slipped quickly into a shop selling T-shirts and touristy kitsch. "Sam?" she muttered under her breath.

She walked slowly by the shop, but didn't see anyone inside who looked like Sam. She continued on, keeping her pace slow as she made her way back to the pub. That was twice she thought she'd seen Sam.

Before she stepped into the pub, she looked behind her, scanning the street, which wasn't packed, but there were enough people that she couldn't be absolutely sure he wasn't there somewhere. Nico had left the restaurant, and their table was empty. She located her scarf, which had slipped to the floor behind her chair, and made her way back to the street. She walked in the opposite direction, pausing to look in shop windows occasionally. Despite the gray day, she could see reflections in the windows. She was facing a display of Christmas party dresses when she saw the man's silhouette in the reflection. She moved to another shop. The display of goods for sale didn't even register; all she saw was the familiar outline mirrored in the window.

She watched for a moment. The man was turned away from her, looking into another shop window. She chewed on her lip for a moment. She could run, try to lose him, but if it was Sam...she let her scarf, which she'd been holding, slip to the ground. As she whipped around to pick it up, she got a good look at the man.

"Sam!" she called as she snatched up her scarf and dodged across the street. She watched him, sparing only a quick look at the traffic, and saw a flash of astonishment that he quickly masked with a smile.

11

"Zoe what a pleasant surprise," Sam said as she reached him.

"I don't think it's much of a surprise. You're following me. Why?"

"Following you? What are you talking about? I have a meeting in half an hour. I'm just killing time until then."

Was she wrong? Impulsively, she took a stab in the dark. "Like you were killing time earlier near the Leicester Square tube station? Like you just happened to be on the same flight to London as I was. That's a lot of coincidences." As soon as the words were out of her mouth, she mentally second-guessed herself. She could almost hear Helen's voice saying, *don't rush to judgment.* Helen was all about measured, thoughtful decisions. Zoe wasn't. She had a sinking feeling. If she'd walked on for a little longer, watched him a bit more, she might have seen him turn into a building for his meeting.

Sam looked at her for a moment, then threw up a hand.

"Okay, look, you're right. That is a lot of coincidences, but I'm not following you now."

"Now?" She edged back a step. Was he FBI? Or—worse—was he working with the guys in the white van? What did she know about Sam, really? He paid his rent on time, spoke with a soft tone, and had gorgeous brown eyes. "You mean you *were* following me?"

Sam ran his hand through his hair. "Zoe, I haven't been completely honest with you."

A fine mist sprinkled down, and the pavement began to darken with the moisture. Zoe took another step back. "Seems to be a pattern with you."

"Don't do that," he said, his expression wounded. "I didn't think you'd even talk to me if you knew the truth."

"So what is the truth now? You're not really in the resale business?"

"No, that is the truth. I swear." He extracted a business card from his wallet. "See? Completely legit."

"Anyone can have business cards printed."

Tiny droplets of water covered his hair and a few clung to his lashes. "Call the number on there. Go ahead. And, you can look up an article in Entrepreneur Magazine about me. It's online. There's a photo there and everything. I do own the companies. And, I work undercover a lot. All that is completely, one hundred percent, true."

Those things would be easy enough to check...if she had Internet. She could look them up at the hotel. "What *isn't* true?"

"It's more an exception."

"Go on." People were picking up their pace, hurrying

around them, as the drizzle thickened. Zoe pushed her ever-inflating hair behind her ears and raised her eyebrows.

"It's about my mother. She invested all her retirement in GRS stock. I'm trying to find out what happened to it."

It took Zoe a second to process his words. "This is about your mother?"

"Carolyn Clark," he said with a nod. "It doesn't matter to me," he added hurriedly. "I can easily cover what she lost, but she's proud and doesn't want to take anything from me. I figured if I could find out where the money went...I could get some answers for her."

"But the FBI is investigating."

"Right. And how long has that investigation been going on?"

Zoe sighed. "I understand that point more than you know."

"I keep telling her that there's not going to be anything left for the investors, but she refuses to believe me. She is holding out, hoping that when the dust settles from the investigation all the shareholders will be reimbursed. You and I both know that's not going to happen. If I can show her that the money is gone, then maybe she'd accept my help."

"And you thought I could provide the answers to what happened to the money?"

He shuffled his feet slightly. "You seemed to be a logical starting point. You were married to Jack Andrews, you still lived with him when all the money went missing, and the FBI was interested in you—I read the papers. I know you went on the run with Andrews last spring. I figured you had to know something."

"But I don't," Zoe said wearily.

"I know that now. I was afraid if I told you about my mom losing her money—that it was the reason I'd made contact with you...well, I was afraid that you wouldn't want to see me."

"Let me get this straight. You moved to Dallas and opened a branch of your business there, intentionally renting an office from me, so you could meet me?"

"It seemed like a good idea at the time. We were getting nothing out of the FBI, and you'd been involved with Jack Andrews. I figured you had to know something. If I got close to you...I might be able to get the inside story. But once I got to know you, I realized you weren't involved."

His face looked so earnest, but she wasn't about to be sidetracked. Those years in the reality entertainment industry had given her a wide streak of skepticism. "So, back to my original question. Why are you following me? If you think I'm not involved, then there's no reason to tag along behind me, much less follow me to London."

Sam looked even more miserable. "I know it looks bad, but it's not like that. It really was a coincidence that we were on the same flight, and I do have business here. In fact, I have a meeting in," he paused to check his watch, "fifteen minutes. Please don't let my initial misguided beliefs ruin...whatever this is between us."

"We don't have anything between us."

"But we could." He leaned in. "You know it's true. Please, let me take you to dinner. Don't ruin what could be the best thing that ever happened. Someday we'll laugh about this."

Zoe stared at him. "No, I don't think so. That's too many lies." She pushed by him in the direction of the tube, then stopped and turned back. He still watched her. "No need to follow me. I'm going to my hotel."

She made straight for the tube station, anger and—yes, she could admit it to herself—hurt that he had an ulterior motive in wanting to get to know her gave her a burst of energy and pushed away the lethargy from the jet lag.

The streetlights had come on and it was fully dark now. The drizzle transitioned to a light rain. She pulled out her umbrella and joined the crowd of workers heading home, her umbrella bumping along in the tide of umbrellas above the pedestrians. She didn't look behind her until she reached the Underground. She paused inside the doorway and shook the raindrops from her umbrella, watching commuters stream into the station. No tall, silver-headed guy with brown eyes in sight. She thought about the flight, Sam's earnest face as he talked about them being more than friends. She made a little growling sound, and a woman who was coming into the station gave her a look, then moved quickly by her.

As she turned to go to the platform, her phone rang. She didn't recognize the number, but answered it, expecting to hear Sam's voice. It was a male voice, but the guy had a British accent. "This is Dave Bent for Jenny Singletarry."

"Oh, hello," Zoe said. "I was afraid you wouldn't get my message."

"Got it right here. You want an interview?"

"Er—yes." Zoe figured she had to keep going with the lie until she was actually face-to-face with the computer guy.

"I have an opening next week. Tuesday at ten."

"Oh. Well. I'm only in London for a few days. Would it be possible to meet soon? Say tomorrow?" Despite Nico's thought that Bent wouldn't be able to help her, Zoe wasn't about to give up on him. She'd take help from anywhere she could find it.

"No. Unfortunately that's impossible."

"I'd really hoped to speak to you as soon as possible."

"Well, unless you can be here in fifteen minutes, you'll have to wait until next week."

He was probably joking, but Zoe said, "I can do that. I'll be right over." She hung up before he could protest. She stepped outside, unfurling the umbrella as she moved against the crowd and quickly retraced her steps to the street where Dave Bent had his office.

Inside his office, the reception area was empty. "Mr. Bent?" Zoe called, looking into the office behind the receptionist desk where a man was zipping his coat. She recognized him from his pictures. He'd gained some weight, but still had the goatee. "You're here." He didn't sound thrilled to see her. "I can give you ten minutes." He waved her toward his desk.

Zoe perched on the edge of a chair that was filled with papers, notebooks, and magazines, hoping she didn't set off an avalanche. Bent moved a laptop case off sheaves of paper covering the desk to the floor and plopped into his chair, still wearing his coat.

She decided to cut to the chase. She licked her lips. "I'm not a reporter. My name is Zoe Hunter."

He gazed at her a moment, then reached for his laptop bag. "In that case—"

"Please hear me out. I think you'll be interested in what I have to say. I figured an interview request was the best way to see you." Zoe felt a prick of guilty conscious. She had lied, exactly what Sam had done. She pushed the thought away to consider later. "I read about your work with the police, how you've played a big role in finding cyber criminals." She figured flattery couldn't hurt.

He nodded and she continued, "I've been caught up in some cyber crime—I didn't take any money or do anything. In fact, I know so little about how these crimes are committed that I want to hire you to prove that I'm innocent."

He tilted his head to the side, and his thick brown hair drooped down over his forehead to the edges of his circular glasses. "And how would I do that?"

"By finding the money that's disappeared from an account. If you can find it—it's not going to be in any account I own—that would clear me, and then the FBI would leave me alone."

He picked up a piece of paper and began to fold it. "Tell me more."

By the time Zoe had finished explaining her situation, Bent had turned the paper into an origami crane. He set the crane on a stack of paper as he asked, "You think Costa is behind the money transfers?"

"I don't know. It seems possible he could be involved."

Bent shrugged. "There are many people who could have done it."

"What are you saying? That it's a hopeless case?"

"No, just not to jump to any conclusions. Costa and your husband's past association, as you so vaguely put it, may be nothing more than a coincidence." He scooted his chair closer to the desk. "I'll need all the information you can give me about the accounts."

"So, you'll look into it?"

"Yes. What are the account numbers?"

"What about your fee?" she asked warily.

He pawed through the papers on his desk. "If I find anything, I will charge you. My secretary will handle the paperwork tomorrow, give you a contract to sign, all that sort of thing. Account numbers?"

Zoe pulled out the file folder and consulted a page at the back where she'd jotted down all Jack's account information, glad she'd kept a copy of it for herself. She'd found it in Jack's things before the multiple searches of his part of the house. She read the first numbers off to him then looked up to find him sitting perfectly still with his eyes closed.

At the pause, his eyes popped open. "Go on."

"Don't you want to write this down?"

"No need. Continue," he said as he closed his eyes again.

"All right." Zoe read off the string of numbers.

She finished and Bent nodded. He reached for his laptop, his thick bangs falling over his glasses. He brushed them out of his face as he came upright with the laptop. He set it up on his desk, powered it up, and then began typing. After a few minutes, Zoe shifted in her chair and said, "Umm, did you have any other questions?"

He glanced up at her. "You're still here? I'll call you if I find anything."

"Oh. Okay." Zoe stood. He was already focused on the computer screen again, his fingers tapping away. "Don't get up. I'll let myself out."

THE pictures came as attachments to an email. Anna was glad Costa was on the phone and didn't notice her intake of breath. Checking his email was a routine part of her job, but she didn't recognize the name of the sender. The subject line of the email was blank, so she'd clicked it open and found the thumbnails of three photos attached to the email. Even in the small pictures, the red hair was unmistakable. Zoe Hunter.

Anna's back was to Costa. She squashed the urge to look over her shoulder at him. He was still on the phone, his voice carrying through the open door that connected their offices. She was careful not to move as she studied the pictures. The first photo showed Zoe Hunter coming out of a London Underground tube station. *What the hell was she doing in London?*

Anna downloaded the first photo and checked the larger resolution. It was definitely the Hunter woman. A date stamp at the bottom corner showed it had been taken only a few hours earlier. She closed the photo, mentally cursing Wade.

The old wooden floorboards creaked behind her. Anna swiveled her chair smoothly to Costa. "Ernesto called while you were on the other line." She motioned to her monitor. "And these came in. Should I forward them to you?"

If Anna hadn't known him so well she would have missed the narrowing of his eyes. He was angry. "Yes," he said casually. "But there is no rush. Take care of this first." He handed her a note and returned to his office, closing the door behind him.

She waited a beat, then hurried to the double-sided fireplace on the connecting wall. It was large enough that she could have stepped inside it without ducking her head. Costa's voice was muffled, but she could still make out a few words. "...don't care...told you...not through Anna."

Anna wasn't surprised that he had kept something from

her. She knew he kept lots of things from her. She moved across the room, avoiding the noisy floorboards as she swiped her phone off the desk then hurried to the narrow window and opened it.

A gust of frigid air engulfed her as she leaned out to get a signal on her cell phone. The thick walls were terrible for reception. Within seconds, her ears, fingers, and nose tingled with the cold.

When Wade answered she said, "What happened?"

"Nothing. We've been sitting here on her house all day. She hasn't gone anywhere. Just debating about going in to get her. Do you think we should?"

"No. She's not there."

"What? She's got to be here. We've been here since seven this morning."

"She must have left last night. She's in London. Get on the next plane. I'll text you her location."

Anna closed the window and was back at her desk in moments, her pink fingers and reddish nose the only sign that she'd been hanging out the window a few moments earlier.

12

The slant of morning sunlight through the curtains revealed that Zoe had gotten plenty of sleep, but she still felt groggy as she rolled over and sat up. Last night, she'd returned from her meeting with Bent, sent a quick email to the mysterious Ares character, and then dropped into bed.

Zoe rubbed her hand across her face, gathered her wild hair into a bundle, and pulled it over one shoulder. She stifled a yawn as she pulled her laptop toward her to check her mail. Nothing from Ares. She was about to shove the covers off and get out of bed, when she remembered the pin board website. She'd logged into it last night and looked at the board Nico had mentioned, but there had been nothing new. She refreshed the page and froze.

"No way," she whispered as she studied the new photo of a mosaic of a dog. She recognized the arrangement of a black dog with a red leash on a white background. It was from a home in Pompeii. The fog of grogginess disappeared as she focused on the mosaic. Jack had posted it. He'd picked something that they had experienced together, Pompeii, and while Nico knew she had visited Pompeii with Jack, only Jack knew how she'd fallen in love with the mosaics. The intricate shading and delicate lines conveyed through small tiles had fascinated her, and she'd spent most of the time in Pompeii hurrying from one house to another, always checking out the mosaics. There was no description under the photo, only a hyperlink to a webpage.

She sat up, crossed her legs, and stared at her computer screen. But what did it mean? Nico had said that whatever Jack posted, she would understand. Sorry, but the picture wasn't exactly speaking to her, at least it wasn't speaking very clearly.

Was Jack in Pompeii? Had the note with the web address only been sent to get her to London so she could find Nico? But then why not just send her the coordinates to Pompeii directly? Why route her through London?

She clicked on the photo and was taken to the pop-up of the picture. She clicked again on the hyperlink, and an article about a traveling exhibit from Pompeii filled the screen. She quickly skimmed the article, which included photos of the black and white dog mosaic as well as other antiquities found in Pompeii. The exhibit was currently at the British Museum.

She threw the covers back and went to shower. A museum wouldn't normally be on her must-see list. Her first choice would be The Tower or the London Eye. However, the British Museum was definitely at the top of her list today.

THE minuscule tiles ranged from shades of gold and deep

brown to light tan and white. Zoe took a few steps back and the tiles merged together into a smooth gradation of color in the wing of the game bird. It sat on a table among the mix of food items that looked as realistic as a photo.

The mosaics were like Impressionistic paintings, Zoe thought. From a distance, the colors blended, but close inspection showed the individual parts, like the brush strokes —or in the case of the mosaics, the individual tiles. Zoe moved on to another item at the exhibit, a fountain tiled in intricate scallops of green, blue, yellow, and red tiles. As Zoe studied the fountain, she felt the gaze of one of the museum's docents on her. Zoe could understand why. There was only so long you could hang around a museum exhibit without attracting attention. As much as she loved the mosaics and the other items from Pompeii, even she was ready to move on. She'd examined every aspect of the exhibit from the well-preserved furniture to the casts of human bodies and their pets, which had been made as the site was excavated.

A large group with a tour guide shifted around her, and Zoe moved on to the next display, the mosaic of the guard dog. It was her third inspection of this particular exhibit. She'd already circulated through the rest of the museum, hitting the highpoints: the Rosetta Stone, the mummies, and the Elgin Marbles. Now, not sure what else to do, she'd returned to the Pompeii area.

One person from the tour group lingered, hovering slightly behind Zoe's right shoulder. With her peripheral vision she could just make out that it was a man a few inches taller than her with a solid build and wavy dark hair in a double-breasted wool coat. They stood in silence for a moment, both looking at the mosaic. With her gaze still focused on the tiny squares, Zoe said, "You couldn't have just sent me an email?"

"My first choice was a singing telegram, but that was out of the question."

A surge of relief shot through her as she heard Jack's voice. "Too showy?

"Unfortunately, yes. And I knew that wouldn't get me any bonus points with you, which I'm sure I need."

"Six months. It's been six months." She couldn't keep the irritation out of her voice as she turned to him. "I was beginning to think you really were dead."

"There are certain people who I need to think exactly that. There's a good reason I've been lying low."

"Why don't you explain it to me."

He stepped back. "Meet me in the Great Court restaurant in five minutes."

Zoe darted after him. There was no way she was letting him out of her sight, but he'd picked the perfect moment to leave. He slipped out the doorway seconds before a new tour group filtered in, blocking her exit. She fought her way through the doorway and found the next room empty except for a man in a brown sweater and a woman holding tightly to a child's hand.

Exasperated, Zoe hurried through the displays and across the central area that had once been an open courtyard but was now topped with a steel and glass roof. Weak sunlight penetrated through a thin sheen of clouds and threw a grid pattern of shadows from the ceiling's steel beams across the court. The museum's circular Reading Room stood at the center of the Great Court, and she trotted up the stairs that wrapped around the curved wall of the Reading Room to the restaurant.

She hustled into the restaurant and spotted Jack at one of the tables at the back near the low wall that separated the restaurant from the area where a few people were strolling, taking in the view of the court below. His coat was over the back of the chair, and he had on a dark suit with a light blue dress shirt and gray tie. The lunch rush was over and there were only a smattering of people at the other tables. He stood as she approached, smiled politely, and pulled out her chair.

That small, reticent smile slowed her approach. She'd been raising her arm to reach for him, to give him a hug or at least a kiss on the cheek like she and Nico had exchanged, but she slipped into the seat instead.

They looked at each other for a moment. At first glance, he looked the same from his silver-blue eyes down to the tiny scar slightly off-center on his chin, but he had dark circles under his eyes. He was also shooting quick glances around the restaurant as well as the walking area that surrounded it. He'd always been one to hold back, be reserved and cautious, but there was an extra layer of wariness overlaying him now.

The waiter approached and placed a mug in front of her and a bottled water in front of Jack. "I ordered you a hot chocolate. They don't have ginger ale."

"Thanks," she said, a little surprised that he'd thought to ask for her favorite drink.

"Do you want anything else?" Jack asked, and Zoe shook her head. She'd had a sandwich in the museum's café earlier. Now her stomach was churning. "Just the drinks for now," Jack said to the hovering waiter, who removed their menus and left.

She smoothed her hand across the white tablecloth. "Quite a place to meet." Her gaze strayed to the rooftop of the ancient temple that they were on eye level with.

"It's quieter up here, less people, but still a public place." The corner of his mouth turned up. "I'm trying to avoid a repeat of last time. Less chance of you punching me here."

"It was a kick to the gut, and I didn't know it was you."

He dipped his head in acknowledgement of her point. "Why did you wait so long to come?"

"I got your package a few days ago." His gaze snapped to her face, and she realized that he wasn't only wary of what was going on around them, he was wary of her, of her reaction. "You thought I intentionally blew you off?" she asked. "I can't believe this. If you wanted me here sooner, you should have used FedEx, not my mother, to send me a package. You know how unreliable she is. You're lucky I got it at all." Some of the tension seemed to go out of him, and he leaned back slightly in his chair.

"There I was," Zoe continued, "sitting on my hands for *months*, waiting for you to contact me. I knew you would... after the way we left things in Italy." She felt her cheeks heat up at the thought of that kiss. She wished her skin wasn't so fair, that it didn't betray her every emotion so transparently. "Didn't you talk to Nico? Didn't he tell you what I said?"

"Nico and I don't talk. It's too dangerous."

"But he said you went to see him in Naples."

"I had to see him face-to-face that one time, but since then we communicate only through the boards. I can't risk contacting him or you via e-mail or snail mail."

"But you sent me that sketch through the mail," Zoe said.

"And that was risky. I could only do that once."

"So the safer thing to do was mail a package to my mom?" Zoe asked. "You know what she's like."

He shrugged. "It was the only thing I could work out. You don't have an office where I could call you anonymously. My only other roundabout ways to contact you were through Helen or your Aunt Amanda, and I knew the Feds would be watching to see if I got in touch with you through them. I didn't know any of your clients, so I couldn't go that route. That left your mom. The fact that you don't interact with her regularly is a plus. I knew she was unreliable. It was a risk I had to take after I escaped in Venice—"

"Escaped? What do you mean *escaped*? No one could find you. They all thought you'd drowned."

Jack watched her a moment. "Who told you I'd drowned?"

"The polizia," she said quickly then stopped, her thoughts whirling. She tilted her head, thinking over those confusing hours. "No. At first, they wouldn't tell me anything. Then later, the next day, they showed me their report that said witnesses saw you go under. It said you didn't resurface." Zoe leaned across the table and lowered her voice. "Are you saying the police took you into custody—secretly—and faked a report? Why would they do that?"

"It wasn't the police who had me. Well, it was at first. I went to them, actually." He laughed. "Ironic, now that I think about it. There I was dripping wet, essentially turning myself in, although I didn't realize it at the time. There were several witnesses who saw me come out of the water. In fact, they pulled me out."

"That's not what the police told me."

"No, they wouldn't, at least not after they got their instructions."

"I'm confused. Who gave them instructions?"

"That's what I've been working out for the last several months."

"Start over from the moment you came out of the water. What happened?"

"Some helpful bystanders bundled me up in blankets—tourists falling into the canals aren't all that unusual—and waited for the police to show up, which they did. They immediately took me off to a local precinct-type place, which I'd expected. There was quite a bit to sort out. They gave me dry clothes and took my statement. They assumed I was a tourist and had one of their officers translate for me. It was simpler for me to speak English. They didn't know I could speak some Italian. They put me in a cell and went to make 'some inquiries.' I figured it could take a few hours to sort it all out, but by the next morning, I was worried. I could hear two of the officers and understood enough of their conversation to know they were transferring me to an address in the city, an abandoned building apparently. Another party would arrive to pick me up after the police left. When the second officer questioned this, he was told to shut up, and forget he'd ever seen me."

"But the report, the witnesses..." Zoe trailed off as she remembered Nico's words about undercurrents and things not being as they appeared. "So you're saying someone, someone powerful, arranged to have you transferred out of Italian police custody?"

"Yes."

"Victor Costa?"

Jack had been doing a quick visual sweep of their surroundings, but his gaze snapped back to her. "How do you know about him?"

"I've been doing a little research of my own. Keep going. I'll tell you later."

"Okay," he said slowly. "Well, I knew I didn't want to find out who wanted me, at least not that way, so during the transfer, I engineered a boat accident and made it look as if I'd drowned. I put on a good show for the spectators—flaying around helplessly as I went under a few times—then I swam under the water as far as I could before coming up for air. I worked my way over to another street without being spotted. This time when some kindly Venetians fished me out of the canal, I didn't go to the police."

"You went to Nico."

"Yes. It took me a while to get to Naples. I had to do it quietly."

"How? You didn't have any money, clothes, or even a passport."

He traced a line on the tablecloth. "I had some strategically placed assets."

"Friends?" Zoe asked, thinking of the assets—people—Jack cultivated in his former spy life.

"A bank account in Geneva."

Zoe threw herself back against her chair. "Terrific. A secret bank account."

"They're not as secure as they once were before the privacy laws changed, but I had to risk it."

"No, I meant the FBI will love that."

"What?"

"Later," Zoe said. "Let's stay focused on your tale here. I'll add my two cents when you're done."

"Tale? You think I'm making this up?"

"Unfortunately, no. Not after this past week, I don't." He frowned. She waved her hand. "You got money from your secret stash and went to see Nico. Then what?"

"Then, Nico and I made a two-pronged plan. His job was to get your ring back. I went after Costa."

Zoe ran her hand along the edge of the tablecloth. "Thanks for that—for getting the ring and sending it to me."

"I'm glad you got it, despite the unreliable courier."

He smiled in a way that made it hard for her to break their gaze. She cleared her throat and looked at the tablecloth as she steered the conversation to Costa. "How could you go after Costa? No one knows where he is."

He raised an eyebrow. "You have done your homework, I see." The waiter circled by. Jack waved him off then leaned forward. "When someone like Costa vanishes, there are always rumors. I've been running them down."

"But he's been 'sighted' all over the world—everywhere from Hong Kong to Argentina. And the whole exercise could be a wild goose chase. It could be someone completely different who wanted you in Venice."

"True, but I figured that I should start with Costa. He's been connected to this from the beginning."

"But why didn't you just come home? Come forward and tell the FBI what happened?"

"Somehow I didn't think I'd be welcomed with open arms. I found out the GRS money had been replaced, but I had no proof that I hadn't taken it in the first place. Then there was the small detail of how I would get there. Showing up with a fake passport would get everything started off on the wrong foot, don't you think? And, finally, there was the whole incident in Italy—why are you smiling?"

"Because that's how I think of it, too—the Italy Incident. I do see your quandary. I'm sure the Italian police would certainly be reluctant to let you go, if you came forward..."

"Any police force in Europe, actually. And, if I surfaced and went to the police, then there was the possibility that the person who arranged for me to be transferred out of police custody would do it again."

"So you went to Hong Kong and Argentina?"

"No, never made it to Hong Kong," Jack said, and Zoe could have sworn there was a wistful tinge to his voice. "I did check out the Argentina possibility. Nothing there. It was in South Africa this summer that I hit pay dirt."

"You found him?"

"Yes." There was a small smile of satisfaction on his face. "I've been following him since then, and now I've got what I need to prove he's involved in some fairly significant crimes."

"Cyber crimes?" Zoe said.

Jack raised an eyebrow. "Are you going to spoil all my surprises?"

"Just a lucky guess on my part. Go on."

Jack pulled a narrow computer flash drive out of the pocket of his wool coat. "I've got a sampling of what Costa has been up to on this. It should be enough to interest the FBI."

"Does it prove you didn't take the money? Or, better yet, does it prove *I* didn't take the money?"

Jack sighed. "Unfortunately, no, but it should be enough to turn their attention from me to Costa."

"So you're hoping for what?"

"A trade." Jack carefully put the flash drive in his coat pocket. "The rest of the information on Costa in exchange for any charges against me—or us, if they're trying to loop you into this, too—dropped regarding the GRS debacle."

Zoe thought of Sato's intense questions. "I don't know if those FBI guys will go for that. You'd better have some amazing stuff on there." Zoe's phone buzzed. "I have to take this. It's about the money."

Dave Bent didn't bother answering Zoe's greeting. "Can you be in my office in half an hour? I need to talk to you."

"You've found something?"

"Yes."

"I can be there." Zoe had no idea if it was even possible to make it from the British Museum to Bent's office in that amount of time, but she wasn't about to tell him she'd wait until tomorrow.

She grabbed her messenger bag. "Come on. We've got to go."

"Where?" Jack asked, but he was already standing, throwing money on the table to cover their drinks.

"To see a cyber crime expert."

13

"You gave all the GRS information—the account numbers, my details, *everything*—to some stranger?" Jack asked, his voice slightly muffled from the thick scarf that he'd wrapped around his neck as they left the museum. It covered his lower face and he'd settled a black newsboy cap low over his forehead.

"No. I gave them to a well-respected expert in criminal cyber activity," Zoe said, waving her arm wildly in an effort to flag down one of the little black taxis outside the museum. "What's going on with that get-up? It's not that cold."

"Keeping a low profile. London is practically the surveillance camera capital of the world." Jack tilted his head toward a nearby building. Zoe squinted and saw three cameras mounted on the corner, their lenses aimed at the intersection.

"So, this expert. What does he do?" Jack asked.

"He's a police consultant." Two taxis whizzed by, their headlights cutting through the growing dusk. She waved more frantically. She wasn't sure how long Bent would wait at his office. It was already past normal office hours.

"The very people I'm trying to avoid."

"I didn't know what else to do." Zoe said, as a taxi stopped just short of them and picked up another couple. "The GRS money is missing."

"No, it was replaced. Banking error."

"It's missing again." As the words sunk in, he closed his eyes briefly. Zoe continued, "I had a visit from the FBI just days ago. They asked if I'd hidden the money in some offshore account. I had to do *something*. I know nothing about high finance and bank transfers. It seemed a good time to contact an expert, especially since this expert happened to be in the same city that your package was sent from."

Jack nodded, stepped to the curb, and raised his arm. A taxi swung out of the traffic and stopped at his side. "Show off," Zoe said as he held the door for her. She gave the address to the driver, and they were off in the mess of stop and go late-evening traffic.

Zoe threw herself back against the seat. "Nico gave me the email address of another cyber guru, of sorts."

Jack raised an eyebrow. "Of sorts?"

"Apparently, Ares operates on the shady side of things."

"Just what I'd expect from Nico. You contacted this Ares character as well?"

"Yes," Zoe said, a trace of defiance in her tone at his frown. "I'm not sitting around waiting anymore. I tried that and look where it got me. I'm in the middle of an FBI investigation—again."

Jack rubbed his hand over his brow. "Look, I'm sorry I wasn't able to get in touch with you sooner. I'm doing my best to get this straightened out. I understand you're frustrated. I am too, but we have to be careful. Do you realize how much ammunition you gave this expert and this Ares guy?" Zoe could see the taxi driver's eyes in the mirror. He was watching them more than he was watching the road.

"I didn't know what else to do. I didn't know you'd show up today. I didn't know about your one-person international quest to bring Costa to justice. I didn't even know for sure if you were still alive." The driver's eyes widened.

Jack noticed the driver's interest and lowered his voice. "I kept my distance to protect you."

Zoe blew out a sigh and watched the lights flick by the window. "I know. But it didn't work very well. Someone tried to pull me off the street into a van while I was jogging." The driver leaned back an inch.

Jack had been glancing out the back window, but now he turned and focused all his attention on her. "What happened?"

"There were two guys in a van. The driver, who had a unibrow and a shaved head, blocked my path while another guy came out of the sliding side door. He was stocky and dark. Hey—" Zoe pointed out the front window at the red brake lights they were flying toward. "Watch out!"

The taxi jerked to a stop, throwing them forward.

"This is close enough," Zoe said.

Jack paid for the taxi distractedly, his attention still on Zoe. The driver sent her a scowl before he pulled away. Jack joined her on the sidewalk, and she continued, "Anyway, once the second guy jumped out—well, that's all it took. I ran for it. I went through that easement in the cul-de-sac."

They paused on the street in front of the building with

Bent's office. "That's not good," Jack said flatly. His gaze swept the street again. "You're sure it wasn't a random thing?"

"I'm sure. The driver definitely checked my face before the other guy jumped out. And, there were two of them. It was planned. It was a quiet time with no one else on the street."

He cursed under his breath.

"I'm fine, by the way. Thanks for asking." Zoe turned to the door.

Jack caught her arm and pulled her back. "I'm glad you're okay," he said. "So glad," he repeated, staring at her intently. I never thought someone would target you." Zoe couldn't look away from his intense silvery blue gaze. "If they'd managed..." His voice trailed off, and her irritation at him receded.

He cleared his throat. "I can't go there. Not now. We have to stay focused. Someone targeted you, which means that either Costa decided to go after you, or...someone else is involved."

His words snapped her out of the warm fuzzy feeling that had been creeping over her. "Why would Costa go after me?"

"To get to me."

"But you're dead. At least, they think you're dead."

"Maybe he knows I'm not."

Zoe stared at him a moment. "Oh, that's bad."

"Yeah. If he knows I'm not dead, does he know I've been tracking him? Maybe that's why he went after you."

Zoe licked her lips. She didn't want to be in anyone's crosshairs. "Have you seen anyone who looked like the two guys I described working for Costa?"

"No, but just because I haven't seen them doesn't mean they don't work for him."

"But what if they're not associated with Costa?"

"That's worse. That would mean there's a new player, and we have no idea who it is."

She shivered and drew the lapels of her coat up to her neck as she glanced around.

The fear must have registered on her face. Jack said, "I doubt they're going to drive up right now. No one was following you in the museum today. I checked."

Zoe appreciated his attempt to make her feel better, but it didn't help. "We don't need a *new* unknown. We've barely got a handle on the old unknowns."

"True," Jack said. "But whatever it is, we'll deal with it. You didn't even know you were in danger, and you handled it. You got away."

"Only because I'm such a good sprinter," Zoe said, grudgingly.

Jack looped her hand through the crook of his arm. "You could always beat me during that last ten yards."

Zoe steered them toward Bent's building. "Add a dose of adrenaline and there was no way he was going to catch me."

"Did you go directly home?"

"And be a sitting duck? No, I took a slight detour and made sure they weren't headed to the house, then I left town. That night."

Jack smiled at her. "You always did have good instincts."

Zoe narrowed her eyes. "Mostly. You threw me off. I completely believed your boring government employee backstory."

"Confidentiality agreement. We've been over this before."

He pulled off the scarf and held the door to the building open. "You know everything now."

"So you say." Zoe stopped even with him in the doorway. "Yet, less than an hour ago you told me you had a secret bank account in Geneva. Are you sure I know *everything*?" The top button of his coat was open, and she was so close to him she noticed the subtle movement of the knot of his tie as it rose and fell with each breath.

"That was it. My last deep, dark secret. You're completely read in on everything. That means you're up-to-date on everything about my situation."

His tie was wrinkled, and she had an almost irresistible urge to smooth it. She fisted her hand, and shoved it into her pocket as she scooted through the entry. "I read spy thrillers. I know the jargon. Okay. So we're going with openness now. Let's keep it that way. None of that 'need to know' nonsense. See, I can do the espionage speak, too."

"Suits me. Which one?" Jack asked, looking at the doors.

"This one." Zoe led the way into the office. "Mr. Bent?" she called as they stepped inside where the faint scent of something rancid filtered through the air. The receptionist desk was empty and the lights were off, but a desk lamp glowed from the interior office, illumining a pile of papers, a steaming teacup beside the desktop computer, a laptop, and the empty rolling chair behind the desk.

"Mr. Bent?" Zoe called again, edging into the office. The smell intensified as soon as she crossed the threshold. As a property manager she'd run across quite a few gross sights and smells, but this one brought back memories of kindergarten and Brice Yardley throwing up all over the carpet during circle time.

Zoe swallowed hard and put a hand to her nose. "Are you okay, Mr. Bent?" Because of the lack of lighting and the spotlight effect of the desk lamp it took her eyes a moment to adjust. "He must still be around here since the office is open. Maybe there's a restroom in the main part of the building?" Zoe said, returning to the receptionist area.

Jack didn't say anything. He rounded the end of the desk with his gaze focused on the floor. Zoe followed, and as soon as she stepped to the side, she saw two sneaker-clad feet.

"Is this Bent?" Jack asked.

The lamp's glow illuminated the pudgy face and the goatee as well as the edge of a puddle under the desk where he'd been sick. His circular glasses hung lopsided from one ear. Zoe's hand went to her mouth. "Yes, that's him. What's wrong?" she asked through her fingers. "Do you think he had a seizure or something?"

"No." Jack touched a hand to Bent's neck, then stood. "He's dead."

They looked at each other for a second. There were so many thoughts running through Zoe's head that she couldn't form a single coherent phrase for a moment. Finally, she said, "What happened? He sounded fine on the phone, and he seemed perfectly healthy when I was here last time."

"I don't know." Jack leaned over and sniffed the steam rising from the teacup, then wrinkled his nose. "I'm not sure, but it could be poison."

Zoe stepped back from the prone body. "Even if it's not poison, he's dead and that means an investigation. Police and crime scene techs." She took another step back and bumped into a chair, which caused an avalanche of paper to engulf her feet. "The account numbers—he had them. They'll find them on his computer. And they'll find out he called me. My phone number will show as an outgoing call." She kicked at the papers on her feet. "They'll trace it all back to me. And with cameras outside on every corner—"

Jack stepped around Bent's legs and gripped Zoe's upper arms. "Zoe, stop." He gave her a little shake. "Look at me." She looked into his silvery blue eyes. "We're going to be okay," he said in a smooth voice, "but we have to be smart and think clearly."

She nodded and got a grip on her surging panic.

"Did you touch anything when you were here before?"

"I don't know."

His grip on her arms tightened. "Think."

"Ow." Zoe rotated her shoulders, and he released her.

"Sorry."

"It's okay. I get it." She blew out a breath. "Let me think. I might have touched the door when I came in. Then I sat on the arm of that chair over there. The one with all the papers in it."

Jack moved to the chair and wiped it down with his scarf. "Did you write down the account numbers for him?"

"No, I read them off to him. He didn't write them down, just closed his eyes and...memorized them, I guess."

Zoe didn't really want to go back around the desk, but she edged over to the laptop. "This is the computer he had open when I gave him the numbers. He was typing on it when I left."

"Okay, we take the laptop." He was following the cord to the outlet as he spoke. "Check the desk for any papers that mention your name or the account numbers."

"You've got to be kidding," Zoe said, but she was already

scanning the stacks of paper. "The good news is that he has terrible handwriting. I don't see anything that I can even decipher."

"Good." Jack wound the computer cord as he came back to the desk, then reached for the laptop.

Zoe put a hand on his arm. "Jack, I don't know. He's dead. We shouldn't interfere in a police investigation. What if they never find out who killed him because we messed with the evidence?"

"If I've learned one thing these last few months, it's that you have to watch out for yourself. Once we get clear of here, we can mail everything back with a nice anonymous letter, if it will make you feel better. There's nothing we're taking that they can't find out, eventually. A computer guy like him will have his files backed-up somewhere. Grab that laptop, and let's get out of here."

Zoe hesitated. "But taking his computer, doesn't that make us look guilty—" she broke off and leaned toward the computer screen. "Wait a minute..."

"What is it?"

"The email that's open—see the name in the FROM line? SERA218@mail.com? That's the email address that Nico gave me for Ares."

14

*Z*oe clicked on the inbox and looked at a few of the emails. "There's my email to Ares, right there."

Jack's eyebrows scrunched together. "You're saying that this cyber crime expert guy is—was—your shady hacker guy, too?"

They both looked down at Bent.

"Not my shady hacker guy," Zoe said. "Nico's shady hacker guy."

Zoe flinched at the sound of shattering glass as shards flew across the room. Something glowing and on fire thudded to the floor in front of the desk. A bottle stuffed with a wad of burning fabric rolled across a pile of papers and bumped into a stack of magazines. Orange and gold flames licked up the stack of magazines, raced along the leg of a near-by chair, and exploded into a column of fire as it consumed the mounds of papers in the seat of the chair. Tendrils of flame shot out across the floor, snaking up and down the piles of paper, igniting them as it spread. Embers flickered in the air of the small room.

It all happened so quickly. One moment Zoe and Jack were talking about email and the next, fire was everywhere. Instinctively, they crouched to avoid the smoke filling the room. Jack stripped off his coat. "Get the laptop," he called as he kicked a pile of paper out of their path. Zoe grabbed the laptop. She ducked her head, pulled her scarf over her nose, and followed Jack.

The fire reached the long fabric drapes on either side of the broken window. The flames raced up the sides and spread to the swag across the top of the window. Jack had been making for the window, but now he switched direction and aimed for the doorway, beating at the fire with his coat to clear a path. Zoe grabbed the tail of his suit coat and scuttled along. How could it be so bright with fire, yet so dark with smoke? A few embers danced through the air and landed on her scarf. She let go of Jack's suit jacket and frantically brushed them away as she moved in the direction she thought Jack had been moving.

She felt the doorframe, the paint melting and warm on her palm and then she was out, gasping for clean air in the tiny reception area beside Jack. "Your coat," she wheezed, and Jack looked down as if he'd forgotten he was holding it. It was a mass of smoldering fabric, the tiny embers already working into the fabric, curling into flames and creeping across the threads. He flung it through the doorway. It landed on one of the stacks of paper that was already blazing. Before they turned away, it was fully engulfed in flames.

Jack reached for her hand. She gripped it, and they

hurried out the door, through the building's entry area, and into the night.

A few people several yards away were moving in the direction of the flames, which were visible through the broken window. Ash and a few embers circled through the air.

Zoe and Jack slipped away, turning down a narrow street. "You okay?" Jack asked as they hurried, putting as much distance between them and the building as possible.

"Yes, I think so," Zoe said, amazed. She ran a hand over her coat. "Only slightly singed, but I'm sure we both smell of smoke."

Sirens cut through the night. "There's no way that anyone will connect us to that fire or trace you to visiting that office, at least until they get to his phone and computer records," Jack said.

Zoe put Bent's laptop in her messenger bag then turned to Jack. "Let me look at you," she said, pulling his arms out and turning him in a circle.

He'd lost his hat, but otherwise looked just the same, except that he was breathing a bit harder than usual. "Do I pass inspection," he asked, grinning.

"Your shoes have a slightly melty look to them, but you'll do." They resumed walking, but then Zoe stopped. "Wait. Your coat. The flash drive was in the pocket."

Jack reached out to pat the pocket where it would have been, if he'd had his coat on. "It's gone, melted into oblivion."

"But you had a copy, right?" It was a statement, not a question. Jack was careful. He was a back-up file kind of guy.

"Of course I have a copy." He rubbed his hand along his jaw. "There's a slight problem, though. It's in Germany."

"DO you have a hotel?" Jack asked as they moved along a residential street. Since they smelled of smoke and made a memorable couple with their sooty clothes, they were trying to keep to the quieter roads.

"Yes, near Victoria Station." Zoe stopped to consult the map in the guidebook.

"Good. That's not far," Jack said, looking over Zoe's shoulder. "How did you make the reservation? Credit card?"

"Yes."

Jack frowned.

"If I'd known I was going to be on the run again when I made the reservation, I would have used cash. But I'm a little short on it right now, which is rather ironic, considering everyone thinks I have a secret bank account."

"We'll have to risk it," Jack said. "We need to get cleaned up. I'm not exactly flush right now, either. I have a couple of hundred on me."

"How can that be? You *do* have a secret bank account."

"Did. It's closed now. I've been using it to pay for the search for Costa." Jack checked the map. "Let's make a quick detour." He led the way toward a bright, busy intersection.

"This is Piccadilly Circus." Zoe hung back when she saw the sign on the Underground, the billboards, and the mass of traffic.

"And it's busy enough that we should be fine as long as we move fast. I have to get some clothes to change into," Jack said.

"You don't have more clothes?" Zoe asked.

"My suitcase is in Left Luggage at the airport. It only has a new shirt and a change of underwear."

"You mean you're not even staying here?" Zoe asked, shifting around people on the sidewalk, which was becoming more crowded as they moved into the bustling area.

"No."

"Well, where are you staying?"

"Currently? In Germany, at Costa's rather bleak castle."

Zoe jerked on his arm and pulled him to a stop in front of a store window displaying the Union Jack on everything from T-shirts to underwear. "You're staying at the same place as Costa?"

"I'm working there, maintaining the grounds."

"How did you get that job?"

"By bribing the last guy who had the job with a large portion of the cash I pulled out of that Swiss bank account. Now, can we stop playing Twenty Questions and get moving?"

"No. I have a few more. Why would you do that? Get so close to Costa? What if he recognized you?"

"I'll explain, but let's keep moving. This place looks as good as any," he said and stepped inside the shop. "I did it to get the info on Costa. I had access to the building, something that I wasn't able to get when he was in a hotel in South Africa." Zoe followed Jack through the crowded aisles with rows of Big Ben replicas, Union Jack flags, and commemorative plates imprinted with everything from pictures of Buckingham Palace to the faces of the royal family.

"He's not going to recognize me because he never sees me. I work the grounds with a thick coat, a hat, and sunglasses when he's home. It's when he and his entourage are away that

I go inside the building and look around. That's how I found the info on the flash drive." He held up a pair of dark pants and a Union Jack T-shirt. "I suppose this will have to do. It's the least flamboyant thing here. Ah—wait."

He plucked a navy windbreaker off the sale rack, then collected a package of underwear and socks along with a new hat, this one a knit stocking cap. Zoe had more clothes to change into in her hotel room, but she doubted she'd be able to get the smoke smell out of her coat and scarf. She picked a royal blue scarf and a dark gray coat. They checked out and were on their way again.

They moved away from the hubbub of the tourists and navigated to the hotel, doing their best to avoid the major roads. Cutting across Green Park, they made their way between the golden, winged Victoria Memorial and Buckingham Palace. Zoe goggled at the gold crests and gold-tipped wrought iron enclosing the palace. Normally, she would have wanted to linger, hoping to see the changing of the guard, but the experience of the last hour made sightseeing pretty low on her list. Getting to the room safely was her top priority.

Once in the room, Zoe tossed the messenger bag on the bed, pulled off her smoky coat, and crossed her arms. "I think I understand how things stand between us. You flew in specifically to meet me," Zoe said. "As soon as you dropped that flash drive with me, you were planning to get out of here, weren't you? You want me to take the evidence to the police in the States."

"You're not a huge fan of the idea. I can tell from your expression."

"No, I'm not. I'm not your courier. You can't just ignore me for months and then expect me to come running to you when I finally get your message."

Jack crossed the room, stopping inches from her. "That package wasn't a summons. I didn't have any evidence to finger Costa until a few days ago." He ran his finger under the chain at the side of her throat and pulled. The ring moved against her chest, seeming to send out a trail of sparks, as he pulled it out from under her shirt. Once it came free from the fabric, he balanced the chain on his finger, and the ring hung suspended between them. "This," he said as he moved his finger and the ring rocked, "was a message...and a question."

"I got the message—that you were alive." She realized she sounded winded, as if she'd finished a 5K. She wanted to back away from his intense gaze and, at the same time, she wanted to move closer to him. "But what was the question?"

Jack rolled the chain between his finger and thumb and focused on it as he said, "Did you want to see me again? If you went to Covent Garden and found Nico, I'd know. If you didn't," he shrugged and let go of the chain. The ring fell heavily into the hollow between her breasts.

"So when I didn't show up...you assumed I was done, that I'd gone back to my life and didn't care what happened to you?"

"That's all I could assume. I didn't know the package had been delayed."

"So when you got the message from Nico that I was here, you thought...what?"

"I didn't know what to think. I hoped you'd reconsidered and would be willing to pitch in to help me out of this rather awkward spot."

"Awkward spot? I think being the target of several police investigations is a bit more than awkward."

"Precarious? Risky? Are those better descriptions?"

"Closer to the truth, anyway." Zoe couldn't help returning his smile. She wasn't normally one to press people to define their thoughts and feelings, but Jack was always so hard to read. "But now that you know I came as soon as I got your package, what do you think?" As soon as she asked the question, she wanted to take it back. It was too revealing.

"It's perfect timing."

He could only mean one thing. Zoe's heart seemed to shrivel. "Right." She threw open her suitcase and dug through the clothes. "For the flash drive. Of course. I'll just change and we can get that taken care of—"

"That is just like you." Jack caught her hand and pulled her to his chest. "You show a glimmer of feeling and then throw the defenses up as fast as you can. I meant, it's perfect timing in several *different* ways."

Now her breathing was totally out of control. She noticed that Jack's wasn't too steady either.

He'd just dipped his head toward hers when there was a knock at the door.

They both froze. "Room service?" Jack whispered.

"No. They don't have room service here," Zoe whispered.

"Were you expecting someone?"

Zoe shook her head and called out, "Yes? Who is it?"

A masculine voice sounded through the door. "Zoe? It's Sam."

"Sam?" Jack asked.

"What's he doing here?" Zoe murmured.

"You know him?"

"He's a friend from Dallas."

"You brought a friend to London with you?" Suddenly there was quite a bit more space between them.

"Of course not. He happened to be on the same flight."

"Zoe?" Sam called again. "Should I come back later?"

"No, it's okay," Zoe yelled then whispered to Jack, "I'll get rid of him. Hide in the bathroom."

Jack looked mulish at that, so she said, "You don't want anyone to know you're here, right?"

Jack looked in the bathroom. "No exit." He headed for the balcony doors.

"I don't even know if those open," Zoe said. "Oh, they do."

She closed the doors behind Jack and did a quick visual sweep of the room. The maid had been in earlier so the bed was made, but her clothes and shoes were scattered across the chair and spilled out of the suitcase. She was by no means a neat person, but the disarray looked tame compared to her bedroom at home. There was no evidence that Jack had been here except the lingering smell of smoke and the bag of new clothes on the bed, which she could have bought herself, so she left them and opened the door.

15

M ort rang the doorbell and studied the straw wreath with orange chrysanthemums. A small woman in her mid-sixties with a cap of brown hair and dark brown eyes opened the door. "Mrs. Baumkirchner?"

"Yes," she said. The aroma of pumpkin wafted through the open door.

"I'm Mort Vazarri with the FBI. I need to ask you a few questions." Unlike some people who shut down when they heard the words "FBI," her dark eyes lit up briefly in what Mort thought was a flare of excitement. He'd seen this reaction, too, but it wasn't as common. She was probably a fan of TV detective shows. She patted the collar of her honey-colored sweater and seemed to tamp down her enthusiasm. "Do you have any identification?"

"Yes, ma'am." Mort produced his badge and identification, which she studied carefully before handing it back.

"You can't be too careful these days."

"I understand. May I come inside?"

"Of course." A timer rang and she said, "Those are my pies. I have to get them. Come on back." She led him through a formal dining room, the table for twelve already set with china and crystal, and into a kitchen that was messy with baking ingredients, bowls, and a Kitchen Aid mixer on the counter.

"Smells delicious," Mort said as she pulled three pies out of the oven and put them on cooling racks. The spice jars arrayed across the counter made Mort feel a little guilty. Kathy was waiting for him to bring the sage home so she could get started with their pies. Did you put sage in pumpkin pies? He didn't know.

"So, what is this about?"

Mort pulled his attention back to Mrs. Baumkirchner. "The silver Camry in the driveway is yours?"

"Yes."

"Did you drive it over to Vinewood yesterday?"

"Where?"

"That's a subdivision near Frisco," Mort explained.

"No. I was here, cleaning. I'm expecting a full house and have to get ready."

"Did your husband drive it yesterday?" Mort had done a little checking on her before he left the office.

"No. My husband is a trucker. Drives for Wal-Mart. He's been on the road for three days. Due back tonight. But I did let my grandson borrow it," she said with a frown. "He told me he was going straight to work, then he'd bring it here. His car is in the shop."

"What's your grandson's name?"

"Al Baumkirchner." Seeing that Mort had taken out his notebook and was writing it down, she amended, "His full name is Oswaldo, but everyone calls him Al. Is there some sort of problem? Is he in trouble?" For the first time, the curiosity was gone, replaced by concern.

"I just need to ask him a few questions as well," Mort said. Technically, the kid hadn't done anything wrong except deceive his grandmother. Following someone for one day didn't exactly qualify as stalking. "Could I get his phone number from you?" Mort didn't want her to call the kid and spook him.

"Yes," she said and consulted a list of numbers taped to the inside of a cabinet door. She read one phone number off to him then said, "But he's out of the country. My son and his wife are taking a Thanksgiving cruise this year. They left last night."

Mort sighed and asked for the location of the closest grocery store.

"TRUCE?" Sam asked after Zoe opened the door.

"Sam, I don't think—"

"Please. Just hear me out, okay?" Sam asked, working his puppy dog eyes.

"No, It's not—"

His nose wrinkled as he leaned toward her, sniffed, then interrupted her. "Did they give you a smoking room?" he asked, looking perplexed.

"Ah, no. I—had an outside table at a pub during dinner," Zoe said, improvising. "Guy next to me smoked like a chimney."

Sam's face fell. "So you've had dinner already? I was hoping to convince you to let me take you to dinner."

Zoe's phone buzzed. It was in the back pocket of her jeans and made her jump. She saw it was Mort calling and said, "I have to take this." Sam waved his hand in a go ahead motion.

Zoe answered as Sam stepped into the room and closed the door. Not what she'd wanted. She should have asked him to wait downstairs in the tiny entrance way. Too late now, though.

"This is Mort Vazarri. Got an update on the silver car."

"Great." Zoe backed up against the dresser. Sam wandered over to the balcony doors and pushed the fabric aside.

"Did you get that?" Mort asked. "Is the connection breaking up?"

"Sorry," Zoe said into the phone. "What was that?"

"The silver car. I spoke with the owner. She says she lent the car to her grandson, an Oswaldo Baumkirchner. Goes by Al."

"Nice view," Sam whispered as he turned back to the room. A thought, a memory, stirred, whispering through Zoe's mind, but it was gone before she could work out what it was.

"The grandson is out of town for Thanksgiving, so you shouldn't have any problems. Just wanted to let you know so you wouldn't worry."

"Thanks," Zoe said and watched as Sam strolled around the end of the bed, mimed drinking a glass of water and stepped into the bathroom.

The sound of running water came from the bath, then the clink of glass on porcelain. "I'll follow up with him after the holiday," Mort continued, "and let you know he says."

"Great. Thanks for letting me know."

"Happy Thanksgiving," Mort said.

"Okay. I mean, Happy Thanksgiving to you, too," Zoe said and hung up.

Sam emerged from the bath, and Zoe said, "Dinner's not going to happen, Sam. Sorry." She opened the door.

"Right. Okay." Sam passed her then turned back. "Are you sure you're okay? You seem...a little edgy."

You would be too if you'd just found a dead man and almost got burned up, Zoe thought, but managed to keep the words inside. Instead, she said, "No, just jetlagged." She practically pushed him out, closed the door, and leaned her forehead against it for a moment before going to open the balcony doors.

It was empty.

"Jack?" she whispered.

"Over here." Zoe jerked her head to the side and saw Jack hugging the wall, his toes perched on a two-inch decorative molding that surrounded a window on the floor below them.

"What are you doing?" she asked, glancing down into the little garden below them, which was empty—thank goodness.

"I believe the technical term is hiding."

Zoe rolled her eyes. "You can stop hiding. He's gone."

Jack didn't move.

"You're not afraid of heights, are you?"

"I'm not fond of them, no," Jack said, his gaze slipping to his toes.

"Look at me," Zoe said, firmly. "Don't look at your feet. It

esses with your mind. That's the first thing I learned in
climbing."

"Since when do you rock climb?"

"You're not the only one with secrets," she said. Figuring
chitchat was a good thing, she continued. "I took an indoor
climbing class and liked it. What you need to do is move your
feet first. Slide them along the ledge. Get them into position.
Then move your hands."

After a second, he inched one foot along. "Good. Now
the other."

He moved closer, but ignored Zoe's outstretched hand
and grabbed the iron railing instead. He vaulted over, blew
out a breath, and moved into the room.

"If you feel that way about heights, why didn't you stay on
the balcony instead of crawling over to the other window?"

"He was moving toward the window, his shadow getting
bigger and bigger. I didn't know that he wouldn't come
outside." He dusted his hands. "So, this Sam guy...who is he?"

Zoe noticed his fingers were trembling, but decided not to
mention it. "So you don't want to explore your fear of
heights?"

"I have a healthy respect for gravity. Let's leave it at that
and focus on Sam. Why did he barge in here?"

She'd been about to tell Jack about Sam following her
and his mother's lost investment, but Jack's almost proprie-
tary tone rankled. "There's really nothing to tell," Zoe said
instead. "He's a businessman. He rents one of my office
suites."

Jack narrowed his eyes. "And he has business in London
at the same time you happen to take a trip there as well. Does
he travel internationally a lot?"

"I don't know. Some, I guess."

Jack narrowed his eyes. "You're upset with him for s.
reason. Don't deny it. I've seen that look aimed at me oft
enough to recognize it."

"Why would I be upset with him? He's just a tenant."

"Is he?"

"What is that supposed to mean?" Zoe asked a flare of
irritation surging through her.

"It's just that he seemed quite at home, coming here unin-
vited, exploring your room, asking you to dinner."

"So what if he asked me to dinner? Why would that
matter to you? We're not married anymore."

Jack looked at her for a long moment then said quietly,
"You're right. I don't have any hold on you." He turned away.
In a formal voice he said, "We need to change out of these
smoky clothes and get moving, just in case the police manage
to link you to Bent." He picked up the bag of new clothes.
"Would you like to shower first?"

"No, you go ahead," she said, "You're faster." He could be
in and out, probably before she found her clothes from the
tangle of shirts and jeans spilling out of her suitcase.

"Fine." He closed the bathroom door. Zoe ignored the
slightly sick feeling in her stomach and rummaged through
her suitcase.

The door opened a few inches, and Jack leaned out. His
chest was bare and he had a towel around his waist. "Answer
this for me if it rings, will you?" He tossed a phone through
the air. She didn't manage to answer because her brain was
stuck on processing the visual of his nice expanse of muscle
and tanned skin. He closed the door and the water came on.

She shook her head briefly. "Focus," she said to herself.

.es. Pack." She grabbed a fitted, long-sleeved white
., a thick gray sweater vest, and a pair of jeans then
oved the rest of her scattered clothes into her suitcase. As
he worked, her thoughts were on the image of the phone
arcing through the air.

That movement stirred a memory...something important.
There was something about it—something besides the
distractingly nice background of a half-naked Jack. She
picked up the phone, tossed it in the air, and caught it a few
times as she paced around the room. She stopped, her eyes
opening wide. "Al," she whispered as the memory connected.

Sam had thrown a set of keys across the office to Al, the
moody teen who worked for Sam. Zoe tapped the phone
against her chin as she paced to the balcony windows. Al had
put the keys on the counter, and Zoe had noticed the key fob
with the initials *O* and *B* engraved in the leather.

Those letters didn't mean anything to her then, but they
did now. They were initials that stood for Al's full name,
Oswaldo, Mort had said, and some long last name that Zoe
couldn't remember because she'd been distracted with Sam's
movements around the room. But it had started with the
letter *B*.

Zoe paced quickly around the end of the bed then
retraced her steps to the balcony windows, her thoughts
racing. Sam had thanked Al as he tossed the keys as if he'd
borrowed Al's car. She remembered that clearly. Did that
mean *Sam* had followed her in the silver car?

16

J ack opened the bathroom door and emerged dressed in his new clothes. He'd bundled his other clothes into the plastic bag. "Your turn."

Zoe, lost in her own thoughts, didn't reply, but murmured, "He lied to me." A fresh surge of anger raced through her. She marched across the tiny space of the room. "He said once he got to know me, he knew I couldn't be involved, but just *a few days ago* he was following me." Did that mean that Sam had followed her to London, too, despite denying it? And if he'd lied about following her, had he lied about his mother's lost investment in GRS? Could she trust *anything* he'd said?

"Who lied to you?"

Zoe started. She hadn't realized she'd spoken aloud. "Never mind."

"Something is wrong. You look pale."

"I always look pale. I'm a fair-skinned red-head." She handed his phone to him and moved to get her clothes.

"You're chewing your bottom lip. You do that when you're worried. You're not a worrier, so I know that if you're worried, I should be worried, too." He blocked her path to the bathroom and stood with his arms crossed. He should have looked comical in his Union Jack T-shirt, but he didn't because his face was so serious. "So, what is it?"

Zoe considered pushing past him into the bathroom without answering, but she couldn't. Questions were tumbling through her mind, and, if there was one thing Jack was, it was cool, collected, and logical.

"Okay," Zoe said with a sigh. "You have no idea how much this annoys me to have to say this, but maybe...I'm wrong about Sam."

Jack's eyebrows flew up. "That's quite an about-face."

"I know," Zoe said, miserably, "but I remembered something that's changed everything." She told him it seemed Sam had borrowed a car from an employee to trail her around Dallas. "And I saw him when I came out of the pub after meeting with Nico. I thought I'd seen Sam earlier, too, so I confronted him. It was too many coincidences—him being on the flight to London and then spotting him twice during the day. He admitted that he opened a branch of his company in Dallas and rented office space from me so he could get to know me. He said his mom lost all her retirement savings in GRS and was too proud to take any help from him. They weren't getting anything from the FBI, and he thought that if he got to know me, he could get some answers. "

"And he said that once he got to know you, he realized you couldn't be involved?"

"Obviously, a lie. He said he really did have business here and a meeting near the pub, but if he was following me in another c a few days ago then he's been lying the whole time." The sh, smiles, the desire to be *close* friends, the invitation to dinner...had that all been an act to stay close to her, to get to know her even better than he did? How embarrassing. Her cheeks heated.

"Let's go back to the first time you noticed anyone following you," Jack said.

"The silver car," Zoe confirmed, glad to focus on another topic.

"You didn't get a good look at the driver?"

"I couldn't see his face, but there was a flash of light-colored hair when he moved. I thought the guy had blond hair. It couldn't have been Al—he has long dark hair—but Sam's hair has gone prematurely silver. It could look light-colored from a distance."

"He's got gray hair?" Jack asked, and Zoe didn't miss that the fact seemed to cheer him.

"Yes. Very distinguished. That's beside the point. Let's see if *anything* he said is true."

She reached for her battered laptop and ran a search for Sam's companies. He'd told her she could find information on-line that would confirm what he told her. There were websites for both Encore and Rebound, which looked genuine. She ran a search for his name combined with the business name and found a couple of articles about him on business and entrepreneurial websites.

She chewed her thumbnail, wishing she had a way to research him further. Mort Vazarri would be the ideal candidate to ask for help, but she didn't see how she could convince him to run a search on Sam Clark without plaining her suspicions, and she didn't want to draw any more attention to herself where the FBI was concerned.

"The websites are generic, but they could be legitimate businesses. It's easy to make yourself look legit on the Internet," Jack said.

Zoe walked away from the computer. She rounded the edge of the bed, went to the balcony windows then turned back as a thought struck her. "Jack, I never gave him my hotel information. How did he know I was here? We only exchanged phone numbers."

"He must have followed you here or—"

Zoe interrupted him. "And, how did he know I was taking an international flight? I didn't tell anyone, not even Helen. Even if he was following me, how likely is it that he'd have had luggage and a passport on him, ready to go?"

"That would be carrying the Boy Scout motto a little far," Jack agreed. "The other explanation is that he's got some sort of tracking device on you."

Zoe crossed the room quickly and slapped the laptop lid closed. "It's got to be on this. I made flight reservations online, and I only made them a few hours before the plane took off. He was at the airport in Newark with his passport, booked on the same international flight. The only way he could have known my flight was if he had access to my computer."

"If he somehow got a keylogger installed, he'd have access to every website you visited, every word you typed." Jack rubbed his hand down over his mouth as he stared at the closed laptop. "There's only one other explanation I can think of, and it's bad."

"What's that?" Zoe asked, afraid she already knew the answer.

"He's with an organization that has the ability to monitor your email and Internet usage."

"Someone like the FBI," Zoe said. Her heartbeat kicked up a notch at the thought.

"Or the CIA...something like that."

They stared at the computer for a second then Zoe grabbed her clothes. "I'll shower so we can get out of here."

LESS than fifteen minutes later, Zoe stood freshly scrubbed near the door, her wet hair twisted up in a clip and covered with her new royal blue scarf, her suitcase by her side.

Jack shoved her smoky clothes into the bag that contained his. "We can't afford to leave them here in case someone makes the connection between the clothes and the fire. We'll have to ditch them."

"We can toss them somewhere along the way. What about my laptop? Do we bring it or leave it?" Zoe asked, glancing toward the bed where they'd left it untouched.

"It could be valuable for misdirection," Jack said, "but if there's any sort of physical tracking on it..."

Zoe sighed. "Leave it. Good thing I've got an online back-up of all my files."

"How very...unlike you."

"Gift from Helen last year. She said it was something I'd never buy for myself." She tilted her head to one side. "You know, traveling with you is very expensive. First, I had to replace my leather messenger bag after Venice, and now I'm going to need a new laptop."

"Once we're out of this mess, I'll gladly buy you a top-of-the-line laptop."

"That's sweet, but you just told me you're out of money. Or, is there another secret bank account?" Zoe asked.

"You're rather fixated on that, aren't you?"

"I'm glad you had a way to survive, but I'm not a big fan of deception. And, don't think I didn't notice that you didn't answer my question."

"Do I have another secret bank account? Unfortunately, no. I guess I'll have to write a book or something to bring in some cash after I clear my name. Maybe I'll team up with your mom and pitch a reality show or something."

"Forget it. I'll buy my own computer," Zoe said quickly. "Okay, let's get going."

Jack blew out a breath. "Right. Let's do it."

He didn't move. Zoe put her hand on the door. "What are you waiting for?"

"Steeling my nerves."

"Why?"

"We can't go out the door. We have to take the balcony."

"What? You're afraid of heights."

"It's the falling, actually, that I fear," he said and squared his shoulders. "But we can't go out the front. Sam might be watching the hotel as well as monitoring your computer."

"But there is no back way. It's just a garden."

"Exactly." Jack clicked off the lights and opened the balcony doors. He waved her through the doors. "You first. You're the experienced climber."

"WE'RE only one floor above the ground floor." Zoe tried to sound encouraging as she looked over the railing to the square of gravel with chairs and pots of ivy below. A fine mist hung in the air, fuzzing the outlines of the trees that ringed the patch of garden. "I'll go down first. Then you can drop the suitcase down to me."

Jack nodded, his face set. She smacked him on the arm. "It's not like you're walking the plank into the ocean. Just a little drop down to the ground."

"Let's get it over with."

"Okay, here goes," Zoe said and stepped over the railing. Balancing on the small ledge, she squatted and gripped the base of the balustrades, which were slick from the moisture in the air. Zoe wiped her hands on her jeans one at a time then took a deep breath and kicked her feet off the ledge. Her arms jerked, taking all her weight.

She dangled there for a moment, trying not to think about how there was no rope in this climb. Her head was below the balcony now, and she could see through the French doors into the small reception area of the hotel. The desk had been unmanned when they arrived. Zoe had nipped behind the desk, retrieved her key, and they'd darted upstairs before anyone saw—or smelled—them, but now there was a young woman perched in the chair, her head turned away toward her computer monitor.

A quick glance down showed the ground was about five feet below her slightly swinging feet. "Hey," Jack whispered, "You said never look down."

"Yeah, well, you know I'm a rebel at heart." Her straining fingers wouldn't last much longer, but even though she was mentally telling herself to let go, her hands remained clamped to the balustrades.

The playfulness went out of Jack's tone as he saw her hesitate. "You want to bend your knees and roll when you land."

"Who's the climbing expert now?" Zoe asked, her words coming out in little huffs.

"Falling expert. I jumped off a playground and broke my leg when I was seven. I know how *not* to do it. Remember, bend your knees. Let them absorb the shock. Go on. You can do it."

Zoe opened her hands, the ground whooshed up, and the gravel bit into her palms.

"You okay? Did you bend your knees?" Jack asked as he lifted the suitcase over the railing.

"I guess." She stood and dusted herself off.

"Ready?"

Zoe glanced at the reception area. The woman was now writing something. "Yeah. Better be quick. We might have some explaining to do, if we're not."

"Okay, here." The suitcase dropped into her arms. The bag of clothes followed almost instantly and tagged her shoulder. Seconds after that, Jack landed softly on the soles of his feet, in a squat inches away from her.

"Impressive," Zoe said.

"Thank God that's over," Jack said, flashing a quick smile. He picked up the suitcase and she took the bag of smoky clothes. There was a gate in the back corner of the garden that led to a small alley lined with trash bins and a few parked scooters. They moved down the alley and into the street.

Zoe glanced around. "Okay. I recognize this street. We're not far from Victoria. We can get to the airport that way."

"We're not going to the airport."

"But your bag. You said you left it there. And didn't you say you had a return ticket?"

"Which I won't be using. We'll take the train. There are more departures. We can get out of London faster and more anonymously."

Zoe nodded, and Jack said, "So no argument? You're coming with me to Germany?"

"What else am I going to do?" Zoe turned down a road, which had a few cars moving along it and some pedestrian traffic. "Stick around here and wait to be questioned by the police? No thank you, I've had enough of that. And if the police locate me here, once my connection to you is known, then that will set off the FBI in Dallas. I want to know what's on Bent's laptop before I do anything. I need all the information I can get—from Bent's laptop and your information—before I deal with any police. No, I'm stuck with you for now," Zoe said.

"You don't have to sound so grim about it," Jack said. "Some women would jump at the chance to tour European capitols."

"It's not like we're on a fourteen-day tour. We're not vacationing; we're on the run."

They took the Victoria line on the Underground to King's Cross, where they pushed the bag of smoky clothes into a trashcan. Then they went to the railway station, St. Pancras, an imposing Victorian building with Gothic-style pointed arches and towers topped with pinnacles. Inside, a curved glass ceiling covered the main concourse, which had a mezzanine level with shops along the side and bridges running across the open space between the two sides.

They found the line for EuroStar tickets. "Better not use a credit card," Jack said.

"Mine would probably be declined anyway," Zoe said, thinking of the airline and hotel charges. They pooled the pounds they had on them to purchase the tickets, cringing at the amount. "Last train of the day to Paris," Jack said.

"We can change there to a sleeper train that will take us to Germany. I think we'll have just enough money."

"If only we'd booked on-line ahead of time," Jack said as they strode through the building.

"Right. I'll be sure to do that next time *before* I find a dead man." Zoe twisted around to take in the arched glass roof overhead and rows of shops as they raced along. "It reminds me of Covent Garden," she said. "Except, of course, that this was a working train station, not one that has been converted into a shopping—" Zoe broke off as a man on his cell phone bumped into her, spinning her sideways. He apologized and went on his way, but Zoe barely heard him. She'd glimpsed a face in the crowd when she'd turned suddenly.

Jack, who was a pace ahead of her, looked back.

Zoe closed the distance between them. "I think I saw Sam."

17

"Where?"

"Behind us. He had on a baseball cap, a brown one. I think it was him."

"Let's find out." Jack moved to a store window, and they pretended to admire the display of watches. "Look in the reflection. Do you see him?"

"No, he's too far away. Let me look over your shoulder," Zoe said and popped up on her tiptoes.

"Don't do that."

"It is him." Zoe dropped down. "It's okay. He didn't see me. He's looking at his phone, but he's moving this way."

Jack grabbed her hand. "Come on. Let's see if we can lose him." They blended in with several people moving up the stairs to the mezzanine level. They crossed to the other side so they could look down through the open area to the main level.

"There he is." Zoe spotted the baseball cap moving toward them. From above, she could see the silver hair at the base of his neck. He kept his head bent over his phone, only glancing up to avoid running into people.

"Let's keep moving," Jack said, and they took off, heading toward him. They came even with Sam and kept walking. Jack caught her arm. "Look at that." Below them, Sam had done a one-eighty and was now trailing along after them, shadowing their movements on the lower level as they walked along the upper level, all the while concentrating on the screen of his phone.

"How did he do that?" Zoe asked. "He didn't look up here."

"He's tracking us."

"Tracking us?" Zoe stopped. "How could he do that?"

"With a real-time GPS tracker. There's got to be one on you or in your stuff somewhere. We've got to keep moving as we look for it."

A real-time GPS tracker? Zoe wouldn't have believed it, except she'd seen the way Sam had turned without hesitation to follow them. And he was still following them. "How— when could he...? Oh, on the plane. He could have done it on the plane while I slept."

"Forget about that now. Let's find the thing first," Jack said. "Where's your phone? That's the most likely place. Maybe he put some sort of tracking app on it."

Zoe laughed. "Right. Not on my phone." She worked it out of her back pocket. "No apps. It barely takes pictures."

Jack took a quick glance at it and handed it back. "That's practically pre-historic in technology years."

The brown cap continued to pace along in their wake. "Could it be on my clothes?"

"I don't think so. It's probably on something you'd always have with you—like your coat or purse."

"We ditched our coats along with the clothes, so it can't be there." Zoe glanced back. "He's coming up the escalator. Aghh. It's got to be in my messenger bag. Come on," she said and moved into a women's clothing store displaying skimpy T-shirts and camisoles. Zoe dumped the contents of her purse on a glass counter that enclosed perfume bottles. She didn't bother pulling out Bent's laptop because she'd only picked it up a few hours earlier—even though it seemed like it had been much longer than that.

A sales lady approached. "May I help you?" she asked doubtfully.

"Just lost my lipstick," Zoe said as she pawed through the receipts and tubes of lip-gloss.

"Well, let me know if you'd like to try our new scent, Drastic."

"Not now, thanks." Zoe pushed her sunglasses, her plane ticket stubs, and her wallet out of the way. "Good grief. There's so much stuff in here, this is the perfect place to hide something," she muttered. Breath mints, a Chinese take-out menu, a bottle of ibuprofen. Jack stepped to the shop door and returned.

"He's on the other side of the mezzanine."

Ear buds with their cords tangled in a hair clip. A case for her sunglasses that she never used. A stack of business cards held together with a rubber band. Three sticks of cinnamon-flavored gum.

"Nothing. Where is it?" Zoe said, sweeping her hand through the stack of stuff. She paused when she picked up her empty sunglass case. There was a thickness at the bottom. She shook it, but nothing came out. She worked her fingers inside and pried out a small black box about the size of a matchbox, but thinner.

"Jack," she said, drawing his attention away from the shop entrance.

She held up the box. He sent her a blinding smile and grabbed it. "Let's see if this is the problem."

Zoe swept the rest of the items into her messenger bag as Jack approached a woman who was leaving the store, her powder blue shopping bag with her new clothes hooked over her elbow. Jack brushed by her and dropped the black box into the open shopping bag. "Slick," Zoe said as he returned to her side.

A few seconds later, Sam strode by, head bent over his phone. He didn't look into the shop, just followed the woman with the powder blue bag. They watched as Sam trailed her down the corridor.

"Thank goodness she didn't head for the EuroStar area."

"Speaking of that," Jack said, "We'd better get over there. Don't want to miss our train."

Zoe couldn't help looking over her shoulder as they took an escalator down to the main level and went to the EuroStar concourse, but she didn't see any brown baseball caps.

They fed their tickets into the automatic ticket gates and the glass panels popped open. "Good thing it's mid-week. We would never have gotten tickets if it were the weekend," Jack said.

Zoe knew he was trying to make conversation to get her down from the jittery nervous feeling that vibrated through her. "No long weekend here," Zoe said, trying to match his easy tone.

Jack looked at her blankly as they lined up for security.

"Tomorrow is Thanksgiving," Zoe said. "At least, it is in the States."

"I'd forgotten," Jack said as they moved through security. An official took a quick glance at their passports then they were through to the departure waiting area. Zoe hadn't expected to have her passport examined before they left London, but it all went so quickly that it was over before she had time to worry. "Well, that was simple," she said. "I guess the police haven't flagged our passports." Jack murmured an agreement as they boarded their train.

Zoe let out a sigh of relief as the train pulled out of the station with no sighting of Sam.

"We'll be in Paris in under three hours," Jack said.

"Let's get something to eat," Zoe said, realizing that she was ravenous. "All this running and hiding has given me an appetite."

"We'd better stick with the café. It will be the cheapest, and we need to keep as much of our cash as possible."

"Fine. Sandwiches it is." They made their way to the café and ordered sandwiches and drinks, which they ate as they stood at the tall tables in the café area. "Did you see anyone...who looked familiar as we passed through the carriages?"

"No," Jack said. "You?"

"No."

"Good."

They ate in silence as London slipped away and was replaced by fields and hedgerows. As they returned to their seats, an announcement stated they were about to enter the Channel Tunnel.

"Hand me Bent's laptop, would you? I'd like to take a look at those emails."

"I hope it's not password protected," Zoe said.

Jack opened the laptop and the screen came to life, exactly as they had left it.

"I can't believe that he wouldn't have some sort of security on his laptop. I mean, he was a hacker, after all. If anyone should know the risks, it would be him."

Jack shrugged. "Cobbler's kids have no shoes and all that. Maybe he had some sort of incredible firewall and virus detection. Maybe he was just foolish. Whatever the reason, I'm glad." Jack settled down to read. Zoe read over his shoulder for a while, but with her full stomach and feeling of safety, her eyelids began to feel heavy.

The train emerged from the Chunnel and her attention was drawn to the slightly rolling French countryside with its smattering of villages, each dominated with a church spire. She felt her eyes drifting closed. She awoke to the general hubbub of talk and motion as people stood and stretched or moved through the aisles. Jack was absorbed in the screen of the laptop. "Incredible," he murmured.

"We're here, Jack."

He glanced up and blinked. "Right." He slammed the laptop closed and shoved it at Zoe.

She stowed it in the messenger bag. "What's wrong with you?"

Jack jerked Zoe's suitcase off the rack at the entrance to the train without answering.

Zoe said, amazed, "You're angry." Jack was rarely angry, and if he was angry, he didn't show it. He hid his emotions, tamping them down inside.

Jack rotated his shoulders as he worked a deep breath in and out of his lungs. "Sorry." People stepped off the train and surged around them. "You're staring at me," he said, irritated.

"It's such an unusual spectacle. Fascinating really. I think I should jot it down on my calendar or something." He closed his eyes but grinned slightly as she continued, "I'm usually the one who flies off the handle, not you. So, what's incredible?" Zoe asked as they turned and walked along the platform.

"He was playing both sides against the middle," Jack said.

"Bent?" Zoe asked, dodging other travelers.

"Yes. Bent—Ares—whatever his current name was—it's all there on the computer. Apparently, he had several email addresses and he downloaded them all to a single email account. Some of the emails are to Bent and some are to Ares. And, if that's not enough, there's a second, completely different account. It was open, but minimized. That's why we didn't see it when we looked at it in his office."

"Who was he on the other email account? Someone totally different?" Zoe asked.

"No, still Ares, but it's the recipient who is more interesting." Jack paused to consult a board with train departure times. "That's the one we want, the sleeper train to Munich, to start. Come on, let's get our tickets and I'll show you what I found."

ANNA had established a habit of taking a smoke break on the wall walk of the castle after dinner, so no one said anything when she picked up her lighter and cigarettes and left the dining room. Costa didn't like the cold, so he wouldn't follow. She stopped by her room to put on her long wool coat. While the drafty rooms of the castle were freezing, they were actually a few degrees warmer than the even more frigid air outdoors.

She took the circular staircase at the end of the hallway, which followed the curve of the tower. At the top, the thick wooden door stuck, but she shoved it open, ducked through the low pointed doorway, and stepped onto the wall walk.

Icy air swept over her cheeks and tossed her hair into her eyes. She shook it away and lit a cigarette, sheltering it from the wind. She took a long drag, then blew out a stream of smoke. Below the castle, at the base of the steep bluff, a handful of lights twinkled in the tiny village of Lintzberg. Beyond, a few lights dotted the motorway, but the rest of the heavily forested countryside was dark, the land rising and dropping steeply under the canopy of stars.

Anna shifted her gaze to the parking lot, a small sweep of open ground directly below her at the base of the castle wall. A second stone wall, this one with massive wrought-iron gates, encircled the whole castle area and edged the cliff, enclosing the parking area.

Satisfied that no one was lingering among the cars below her, she twisted around and turned her attention to the courtyard inside the castle. The far side of the castle was in ruins with only a section of one of the interior walls left standing. Three stories of stone jutted up against the night sky, the stars visible through rows of narrow windows. Nothing moved in the courtyard. Anna took out her phone and called Wade.

When he answered she kept her voice low, but her tone was sharp. "Finally. Why didn't you answer earlier?"

"Now, Anna, don't get mad—"

She rubbed her forehead with the heel of the hand that held the cigarette. "No names! How many times do I have to tell you?"

"Right. Sorry. Anyway, I've got some bad news. I can't go to London."

"Why not?"

"Haven't got a passport."

"Well, get one."

"Can't. It takes weeks and weeks. You have to fill out a form and send it off. Not to mention the picture..."

"Not a real one. Get a fake passport, you idiot."

There was a pause. "I don't think that would be right."

"What?"

"Traveling on a fake passport...that could get me into a lot of trouble. Federal offense and all. I mean, I don't know for sure, but I bet it's a crime."

Anna flung her cigarette butt to the stone path and spoke through gritted teeth. "So kidnapping is okay, but you draw the line at using a fake passport?"

"See, I've been thinking. This hasn't gone the way we thought it would, has it? It's gotten so complicated. I think I better bow out."

"You don't mean that. If this is an attempt to get a larger share, you can forget it."

"Sorry, Anna. Don't call again. I won't answer."

"Don't you dare—"

He cut her off. "It's been real."

A dial tone sounded in her ear. She hit redial, but he didn't answer. She hung-up on the voicemail message, redialed again. Voicemail.

Anna swung around toward the village and the forest. She was so angry she wanted to throw something. Her fingers clinched around the phone. No, that would be stupid. She shoved it in her pocket and worked to calm her breathing. She never should have counted on Wade. He wasn't reliable, but he was the best she could come up with on short notice. She paced a few steps along the narrow walk. What would she do now?

She knew Costa well enough to know that he liked her, but he didn't love her. Someday—either in a few weeks or a few years—he would move on to someone else. She already saw signs of his waning interest. What would she do when he moved on? She had nowhere to go, hardly any money. The ransom money would have set her up nicely, but now...she blinked and swallowed the thickness in her throat. Now she had nothing.

She needed to get inside. Soon, Costa would send Ernesto to look for her, if she didn't return. She wiped a finger under each eye and raised her chin to the chilly air. She would find something, some way to survive.

She went inside and met Costa in the hallway. He caught her frigid fingers in his hands. "You should smoke inside. You know I do not mind."

"But I like the stars and the cold doesn't bother me. Remember, I wanted to go somewhere where it felt like winter."

"I do not understand this fondness for the cold. The sun, yes. Longing for warmth makes sense, but not this," he said, raising her pink fingers. He chaffed his hands over hers, then said, "I had Ernesto build a fire in the drawing room. I will be back shortly." She walked a few steps, but turned to him when he called her name.

His eyebrows lowered over his squinting eyes, he asked, "Michigan?"

"Not even close." She threw him a flirty smile before she resumed walking. She knew better than to ask what he was going to do.

She entered the drawing room and warmed her hands at the fire for a moment, then reached in her pocket for a cigarette. She needed another one. Her plans had been smashed beyond repair, after all. She patted her coat pocket and realized she must have left her lighter on the stone parapet. She retraced her steps to the top of the castle, hurried through the door and onto the wall walk. Her lighter rested on the stone. She picked it up and turned to go, but a flicker of movement in the car park caught her attention.

She frowned. It was Costa, moving quickly through the cars. Was he leaving? He opened the trunk of the black Mercedes, removed a box, then closed the trunk and perched on the bumper as he opened the box and removed something. The lighting was too dim for Anna to see what it was, but after working with it a few moments, he transferred to the driver's seat and turned on the lights to the car, but didn't start the engine.

Anna leaned on the parapet and tried to quiet her breathing. He'd left the driver's door open. One foot rested on the ground outside the car as he worked with whatever he'd taken out of the box. Because he was directly below her, she couldn't see him. The roof of the car blocked him from her view, but his words floated up to her through the clear night air.

"I do not like phone calls," he said, his tone matching the icy air. After a moment, he said, "Lost her?"

She couldn't make out his next words, but she could tell he was angry. Finally, he said, "Leave it. Forget about her. Did you take care of the loose end? What about the package? Do you have it? Good. Then get back here. Tonight." His voice had softened as he spoke, and Anna leaned over at the waist to hear him. Costa was one of those people who didn't get louder when he got angry—he got quieter. She'd learned that it was best to avoid him when he spoke as he did now.

She swallowed, suddenly aware of her precarious position. She was careful not to bump any lose stone that might alert him. His words were barely a whisper as he said, "Do not lose anything else."

The growl of the car engine filled the night. Costa got out of the car, placed the cell phone beneath the front tire, then backed over it. He threw the car into park. Before he'd turned the car off, Anna had pushed through the thick wooden door.

18

Zoe and Jack had enough cash to buy the night train tickets, but had to purchase one of the more expensive deluxe two-bed sleepers because it was all that was left. Once in their compartment, Zoe tossed her messenger bag on one of the two seats and took out Bent's laptop. "So let me see these email accounts."

He opened two windows that had been minimized.

The first account had a mix of emails with most addressed to Bent Consulting and only a few to Ares. "I don't know much about what a computer expert in cyber security does, but these emails to Bent Consulting look fairly normal." She skimmed through the subject lines, which contained an invitation to speak at a cyber security conference, an interview request from a London newspaper, and follow-up questions from an inspector about a case on which Bent had been consulted. One with the name Costa in the subject line caught her attention. In reply to a query on tracing an IP address, Bent had written, "Nothing—sorry. No go on addy. I'll keep looking. Don't hold out hope."

Zoe switched to the emails addressed to Ares, the one with the address Nico had given her. She squinted at the email address, SERA218@mail.com. She looked up quickly. "Hey, I get it. Sera is Ares spelled backward."

Jack tilted his head. "You're right. I hadn't noticed that."

"That's about all I can figure out about these." Zoe couldn't decipher the replies. They looked like gibberish— just numbers and letters without spaces. She supposed it could be some sort of code, or maybe the bodies of the emails were encrypted.

She switched to the other email account. After a few seconds of scrolling and clicking, she looked up. "There aren't any emails in this account at all. Nothing sent or received."

Jack put her small rolling suitcase in the rack above the door. "Check the drafts folder," he said over his shoulder.

There were messages—plenty of messages.

"Why would someone compose draft emails, but never send them?" She didn't wait for him to answer, but went back to reading the emails.

Jack leaned against the window. "Because someone else had the log-in info for the email account. That way, two people could each read and reply to the emails without actually sending them. It's a common technique to avoid someone intercepting emails. Terror groups use it. Teenagers, too." His face worried her. There had been a brief lull when they were getting the tickets and finding the train that he'd looked normal, but now he was back to being stressed. She could tell there was something bad in the rest of the emails.

The communication was hard to follow because there

were no names in the headings and the subject lines were often blank, but there was a definite feel of an exchange between two different people. One person sent short abrupt commands in full sentences with correct grammar and punctuation. The other person replied in short phrases and used abbreviations and punctuation haphazardly, a copy editor's nightmare. "This one with the choppy phrases and abbreviations is probably Bent," Zoe said. "The style is similar to his other emails, the ones he signed with his Bent Consulting email signature."

"I agree," Jack said.

"So who is the officious Mr. Proper Grammar?"

Jack raised an eyebrow. "Who do you think?"

"No, not Costa."

"The tone fits what I've seen of Costa's business correspondence. The info I collected in Germany has a similar style." The train pulled out of the station as he spoke, but neither one of them was interested in looking at the city lights as they left Paris.

"But lots of people use a formal tone in business. Aren't you stretching a bit? Seeing Costa everywhere? Wouldn't it be too much of a coincidence?"

"No, it would be a neat little circle that I can see Costa working to his advantage. Costa pays off the leading consultant who's supposed to help the police track him. In his position, Bent could keep the investigation away from Costa, or if he couldn't do that, then he could at least keep Costa appraised about how close the police were to him."

"And that would allow Costa to stay one step ahead of the investigators," Zoe acknowledged. "It would explain how he's always just slipping out of their reach."

"Keep reading. I think you'll agree with me by the time you get to the end of the draft emails."

She scanned the emails, working her way backward. Jack left the compartment, but she barely noticed. After an hour, she'd read nearly all the emails that went back over two years.

Jack returned to the compartment, and she said, "I don't see any names of people, but these words like Evergreen and Silver Fox, they look like a code."

"They are. I found the same thing in the data I have on Costa. Silver Fox was a scam involving retirement accounts." Jack ran a hand along his jawline. "One that I haven't seen until today is Evergreen. Take a closer look at those."

"There's quite a few," she said as she clicked through the first ones. By the time she'd read the first twenty or so, she frowned. "These dates, and what they're discussing. It almost sounds like they're talking about GRS." Zoe looked up. "You don't think...Evergreen isn't...?"

"Me? Afraid so. Well, actually I think it refers to GRS in particular. There's a bank account number listed in one of the exchanges and it's the account number for GRS's business account."

The porter arrived and folded away the seats then lowered the bed while Zoe read the next emails, skimming through the text, reading impatiently, but with a growing sense of unease. When he left, Zoe sat on the lower bed.

"Jack, these emails..." she trailed off, almost not believing what she'd read. But it was there in black and white, a neatly drafted plan to ruin a man's life—Jack's life. "I can see why you were angry. You were deceived."

"I was stupid." His voice had turned serious. He leaned

against the wall and sighed with disappointment. "Those draft emails explain a lot of things I ignored or wrote off as coincidence. They fill in a lot of gaps."

"But it says you were set up—from the very beginning."

Jack shrugged. "It's all there. Look at the emails—somehow Costa found out I was anxious to start the company, but had zero funds. He bet that I would barely need convincing to take Connor on as a partner. I'd be so glad that I had a backer that I wouldn't look too closely at the capital. And he was right. I never wanted to delve too deeply into where Connor got it. I was just glad he had the money. You saw his place in Vegas last year. There's no way he had that kind of seed money stashed somewhere for a business and lived in that pigsty."

"I'll give you that," Zoe conceded, remembering Connor's tiny, filthy apartment, "But the rest of it. It's so unbelievable. You really think Costa set up this elaborate scheme? That he hired Connor to basically impersonate a businessman and gave him cash to run the company?"

"To run the *scam*," Jack corrected. "It was a classic long con."

"That's...I don't know...Machiavellian."

"Look at the results," Jack said. "In the end, after you strip away me and Connor, you've got a pump-and-dump stock scheme. The investors were the marks along with Connor and me. The investors put in money, Connor worked to inflate the price through all those phony posts on stock message boards, then the money was yanked when the stock was at the high point. After the stock tanked, Connor and I got blamed, and Mr. Anonymous had the Bent-slash-Ares guy manipulate the money so that it disappeared, leaving me as the scapegoat. If I weren't in the middle of it, I'd have to admire it. It's brilliant."

"I wouldn't call it brilliant. Devious. Cunning. Something along those lines."

Zoe ran her finger along the edge of the laptop. "I wonder why Bent called me. And why would he take 'my case' in the first place? I'm sure he recognized your name and Costa's.

"He probably saw an opportunity to fleece you—take your money, but give you no real information."

"He said he'd only charge me if he found something, but it looks like he wasn't the most honest guy on the planet." Zoe sat up straighter. "I just thought of this—do you think he told Costa I hired him?"

Jack shook his head. "There was nothing about that in the emails, and those two seemed to communicate exclusively by email."

"So you don't think Costa had anything to do with Bent's death and the fire?"

"Which we were so conveniently almost caught in? I don't know. It could have been Costa, or it may have been someone else from the Ares side of his life. It looks like he dealt with a lot of shady characters."

Zoe chewed on her lip for a moment. "Jack, there's another thing about these emails."

"Don't tell me you've found another email account on that laptop."

"No." Zoe smiled feebly. "I'd almost take another email account over what I just realized."

"That sounds ominous."

"Once the police find these draft emails, they'll think we have an excellent motive for killing Bent."

ANNA waited until after midnight to slip out of bed. Costa lay motionless beside her, his breathing heavy. He wouldn't miss her.

She knew that Costa could not resist panettone, an Italian sweetbread dessert with raisins and candied fruits. That's why she put the powder from the crushed decongestants in his slice of the cake. The few times she'd seen him sick with a cold, the medicine had made him so drowsy that he could barely open his eyes for several hours.

Wrapped in her thick robe, she took her cigarettes and walked down the chilly hallway into the offices. She went to his desk. He was keeping something from her and she wanted—no, she needed—to know what it was.

He didn't think she knew his habits, but she was more observant than he realized. Always security conscious and wary of hackers and investigators, she knew Costa changed his passwords to his accounts each week. She also knew he made a note of his new passwords on an index card and kept it under his blotter, religiously shredding the old index card himself each Monday morning.

She consulted the index card, found the password for his computer and then for his private email account, and replaced the index card. The screen came to life, and she opened a special program on the computer that she had installed.

Costa shied away from using his computer, but he couldn't avoid it completely. When he did use it, he consistently deleted his Internet browsing history each day, but the handy program she'd installed kept a history of every site visited and all search words entered. She skimmed through links to banks, financial sites, and news until she came to several unusual links about art.

She clicked on them, a smile growing as she read about a Monet oil painting called *Marine*. There was only one reason a man like Costa researched artwork. Either he was going to steal it, or he was going to buy it. Since the painting was already stolen, Anna was sure he intended to buy it. Probably with the money from the pump-and-dump stock scheme he'd engineered through Jack Andrews.

He'd wanted to set Jack up as the fall guy for the transaction. He had some sort of personal vendetta with Andrews; that was why he'd waited for Andrews to resurface, to make sure he was actually dead. If he had resurfaced, Anna didn't doubt that Andrews would be the scapegoat. With Andrews dead, Costa intended to put the blame on Jack's ex-wife. Costa was not a man you wanted to cross. His hatred extended to the families of his enemies.

She would have to be very careful, but she was sure the package Costa had mentioned on the phone tonight was this painting. She also found an order for a leather tube described as "perfect for transporting delicate oversized papers such as blueprints and artwork."

She couldn't find any new emails, even in the draft folders that she knew Costa used, so she opened the history on the print queue. A few changes to the preferences on the printer menu, and she had a record of every item that Costa printed. She clicked on the single item listed, "letter.doc," and printed her own copy, then deleted it from the history. She knew it was odd when she spotted Costa alone in the village a few days ago, walking quickly away from a post box. He rarely ventured out of the castle alone, and he never went to the village on his own.

Anna took the document from the printer. A letter, how antiquated. No email trail and no phone record either to give away the connection between Costa and the recipient. She leaned back in the chair, little puffs of white air escaping as she breathed. There was a way out after all, and it was even simpler than her first plan.

IT was late Thursday afternoon by the time Zoe and Jack arrived in Lintzberg, and, with the early twilight of fall, the sun had slipped below the horizon leaving only the orange wash of sunset tinting the high points of the forested hills above the town. Situated in a hollow of land below a high precipice, the village was already in darkness, but lights shined from inside the windows of homes and shops. Glowing white Christmas lights hung across the main road, which curved through the town between rows of two-story stucco-faced buildings painted white, gray, and cream.

Zoe pushed her chilly hands deeper into her pockets, glad that she didn't have to expose one hand to the cold to pull her suitcase. They'd left it in the luggage storage area at the train station. At least the buildings sheltered them from the icy wind that had sliced through the fibers of Zoe's coat the moment they emerged from the train.

The little town was busy with activity as small cars zipped by them on the narrow road, and people moved along the sidewalk, some carrying baskets filled with the day's shopping.

"How far is your car?" Zoe asked as they trudged along.

"Up there." Jack pointed to the outcropping of rock, a dark black blob against the star-speckled sky. "I left it in the castle's parking lot. I didn't want to draw anyone's attention. It's been there for weeks. If it was suddenly gone, it might arouse suspicion," Jack said, moving on through the crowd of people wearing heavy coats and scarves, their breath making little wispy clouds as they exhaled.

Zoe rubbed her hand across her eyes. "Of course, it's at the top of a mountain," she muttered.

Jack turned to her. "Say something?"

"Just ignore me. I'm tired and crabby. And worried," she added, thinking of Bent's motionless body.

They'd spent most of the time on the train from Paris going over the draft emails and searching the computer for more information, but they hadn't found anything else as revealing as the emails. They'd arrived in Stuttgart, Germany at four in the morning then switched to the first of two regional trains that brought them to Lintzberg.

Their train had been delayed out of Stuttgart, causing them to miss their next one, and they'd had to spend two hours in a small German hamlet that Zoe couldn't even remember the name of, much less pronounce. Her grasp of one foreign language, Spanish, had been basic, but enough that when she was in Italy she could decipher some of the Italian signs, even catch a few words of Italian, but she had no clue about the German words or signs. The incomprehensible strings of letters made her feel completely out of her element, despite having edited several German guidebooks.

She knew part of her discombobulated feeling came from lack of sleep. She'd tried to catch a few hours sleep on the regional trains, but there had been too many questions circulating through her mind. She hadn't been able to relax. Unlike Jack, who reclined his seat, crossed his arms, and was snoring in about five seconds.

"Come on, where's the sight-seeing fanatic I know? I thought you'd love this—a quaint, German village at Christmas."

"I can't take in quaint right now."

"Let's get some food. We've got time," Jack said as the road widened into an open cobblestoned area with a towering Christmas tree decorated in red stars and Santa hats. Small shops ringed three sides of the open area and a brick church with a gothic-style spire dominated the fourth side.

Zoe led the way to an open-air vendor who was set up near the Christmas tree. A woman was leaving with a cup of what looked like hot chocolate. Zoe pointed to the cup and held up two fingers, after glancing at Jack with raised eyebrows to see if he wanted one.

"I'm afraid that's the extent of my German communication abilities right now. I can't remember anything beyond bitte and danka."

"You got the job done. That's all that matters." Jack handed some money that they'd exchanged in one of the train stations to the man behind the counter. "Do you want one of those?" Jack asked nodding to a customer standing at one of the high tables eating a sausage on a stick.

"Sure. When in Rome and all that."

A few minutes later, Jack handed her a sausage and they moved to a tall table.

"It's good," Zoe pronounced after a few bites. "Spicy, but

good. Of course, I'm starving, so I'd probably down some cardboard right now and say it was fantastic."

"This is definitely better than cardboard." Jack held out a thin pancake that had been folded in half then folded over again. "Try it. It's a crepe filled with Nutella."

Zoe took a bite and closed her eyes in bliss as she chewed. "I think I need one of those, too," she said. She opened her eyes and realized Jack was smiling, his eyes half-lowered. She looked away quickly and felt her cheeks heat up despite the freezing air.

"Have another bite," Jack said in a deep, almost lazy tone that made her stomach do a little flip.

"I—ah—thanks, but I'm full now." Zoe looked around for something to distract her from the crazy feelings she was having. What was it about Jack? How did he do this to her? He'd been gone for months, and she'd decided to keep all her options open, but then he offers her a bite of food, and she practically needed to sit down because her knees felt so weak? Her knees had no business going all wobbly on her. They had other things, problems—big problems—to sort out. Would the information Jack had convince the police they were innocent victims in this mess? Would they believe Jack and she had nothing to do with Bent's death and the fire at his office?

"So where are these files again?" Zoe asked, her voice brisk.

"Back to business? You're not usually so tightly focused."

"I'm focused on getting the flash drive. Our whole reason for being here."

He sighed with disappointment. "If you insist. The drive is

in my room." He nodded at the dark precipice overhead. "In the castle."

"So tell me about the castle." Zoe sipped her hot chocolate. "I can't even see it."

Jack finished the crepe and wiped his mouth with a thin paper napkin before he spoke. "It's set back a few feet from the edge. You'd be able to see one of the towers during the day. It was once a triangular fortress with towers at each corner. It was shaped like an isosceles triangle, two long walls and one short one. The short wall looked out over the valley. Today, only the short wall and the tower connecting it to one of the longer walls are standing. The rest of the place is in ruins. Some wealthy industrialist bought it in the eighteen-hundreds and restored the tower and some of the buildings that adjoin the standing wall."

"Is it a tourist site? Can you visit it?"

"Not now. It used to be, but Costa bought it and closed the livable portion to visitors. The ruins are open from June to August. There's quite a bit of rumbling in the town about the reclusive owner. Most people here have never seen him, only the Mercedes with tinted windows that he drives to and from."

"How could he buy a castle when he's a wanted criminal?"

"He probably had an attorney act on his behalf during the negotiation. I'm sure that the title is in an alias, or he's bought off any local officials so they will look the other way and protect him from potential investigation."

"And you maintain the grounds there?"

"Yes. Temporarily. The prior groundskeeper had an accident with a chainsaw. Cut up his leg. He's going to be fine, but he's afraid that if his reclusive employer found out about his diminished work abilities he might lose his job. He was more than happy to have someone step in and fill his shoes."

"Without his employer knowing it?"

Jack nodded. "Fortunately, the only other staff is a cook-slash-housekeeper who comes in from the village when Costa is in residence, and she happens to be the permanent groundskeeper's aunt, so she won't give the game away. She wants her nephew to keep his job."

"And how are your grounds-keeping skills?" Zoe asked, thinking of the minimal yard work Jack had done at home.

"Let's just say it's a good thing it's winter," Jack conceded. "The heavy pruning is finished, and there's no mowing this time of year. I open the gate in the morning, do minor repairs and maintenance during the day, and lock up at night."

"Sounds more like a general handyman," Zoe said. "Don't think I'll forget this. I've got a kitchen ceiling that needs some drywall. Sounds like you're just the man for it."

"Believe me, I'd rather be there than here, avoiding Costa."

"And have you been able to do that? Avoid him?"

"Yes. It's not too hard. He stays mostly in the refurbished living quarters on the second and third floor. My room is tiny. I think it was originally a storage room. Either that or part of the dungeon. I make sure Costa and his entourage are out before I venture up to their rooms."

"His entourage?"

"Only two people. Ernesto Moretti, an oversized, no-neck kind of guy. Chauffeur-slash-bodyguard. And, Anna Whit-more, his American secretary-slash-mistress."

"Wow. He must have been hit hard by the downturn in

the economy. Does everyone who works for him have to do double duty?"

"Tough times everywhere, I guess, even for criminals. No, seriously, he's just being smart. A large group of people would attract more attention. He can move quickly, and he limits the potential for leaks when he only has a few people around him."

"So we walk to the top of the mountain, get the flash drive with the files, and then get it to the FBI," Zoe said as she gazed across the square at the people shopping or pausing for a hot drink.

"You take it to the FBI. I stay here and keep an eye on Costa."

"I don't like that part. Nothing good ever seems to happen when we split up."

"Not what I want to do either, but I have to stay. If Costa disappears again, we're right back where we were."

"No," Zoe countered. "We have evidence of what he's done. With the draft emails and your info, we can prove we weren't involved in the pump-and-dump scam."

"But our position is even stronger, if we can pinpoint where Costa is."

Zoe knew he was right, so she didn't argue with him. Instead she said, "This really is a quaint little town." Now that she'd had some food and the hot chocolate had warmed her, she could appreciate her surroundings.

Small evergreen trees in pots edged the street. Single gold bows were tied at the top and streamers of ribbons draped from the bows straight to the ground. Garlands threaded with lights hung in scallops from balconies and storefronts.

She frowned as she caught sight of a familiar silver-headed figure. "That can't be..." she murmured.

Jack's relaxed attitude vanished. "What?"

"There, on the far side of the open area where the cars are creeping through the pedestrians. Is that Sam?"

"Which car?"

"The small one."

"They're all small."

"The smallest one. Blue." Zoe pointed. "The one that's turning onto that street beyond the church." As the car turned, she got a good look at the driver's profile. "That *is* Sam. How can he be here? Surely there's not *another* tracker on us."

"No, I don't think so," Jack said, as he reached for her hand. They hurried away from the exposed table, merging into a group of people crossing to the other side of the square. "He didn't seem to be looking for us—or anyone else, for that matter."

"You're right. He didn't even scan the crowds. All he was interested in was turning onto this road," Zoe said as they left the open area and began climbing up the steeply inclining road. "Where does this go, do you know?"

Jack glanced up. "The castle."

19

Anna was browsing on-line, looking at handbags and considering which Louis Vuitton bag she would tell Costa she wanted for Christmas when she heard the commotion, feet moving rapidly through the hall and the slam of doors. It had been a fairly busy day, and she had been careful to act as she always did, and not vary her routine. Costa had seemed exactly the same, so she didn't think she'd given herself away.

She left the drawing room and followed the sounds of the raised voices to the office then gently opened the door a crack. Costa stood, his arms braced on the desktop. Another man with gray hair, but a young face stood on the other side of the desk.

Anna hadn't seen him before, but she'd bet this was Sam, the American who had been monitoring Jack Andrew's ex-wife and watching for Jack. If he was here, things were coming to a head.

"I told you," he was saying, "I did everything possible to

keep track of her. I had the tracker on her car and when the battery went out on it, I trailed her myself in a car she wouldn't recognize. And, I planted the tracker in her bag when she went to London."

"And yet," Costa said, his voice soft, "You still lost her."

"But I did everything else."

"I am sure you did your best. However, I am disappoint-ed." Anna swallowed, knowing from his tone that the man had fallen far short of what Costa expected. She'd heard him use that tone and those exact words with Henri, who always leered at her hungrily when he thought she wasn't looking. She'd been shocked when she heard Henri was dead. He'd been mugged in the streets of Naples, his throat slit and his wallet missing. Costa had shrugged.

"I took care of Bent," the man continued in a somewhat belligerent tone that made Anna's heart pound. No one talked to Costa like that.

"That was more important," the man insisted. "You don't need her."

Costa stared at him a long moment, then crossed his arms and paced to the side of the room. "How did you take care of Bent?" he asked, his gaze on the rug.

"Poison."

Costa swung toward him, his eyebrows raised.

The other man shrugged. "I like a little variety. You don't need to worry. I set his office on fire. It was stuffed full of papers and books. Went up in less than two minutes. There will be no evidence."

Anna saw Costa shake his head slightly and knew he was even more displeased. The other man didn't pick up on the small movement. He settled into a chair across from the desk and stretched out his legs. "I figure, I completed this job as well as I could, considering that you sent another crew and spooked her."

"What?"

"In Dallas, the two men who tried to snatch her. I was shadowing her and saw them. You should have told me you wanted me to bring her in, and I would have done it. I had her eating out of my hand. I could have proposed a romantic European getaway, and she would have tripped over her own feet to get to the airport."

"I see."

Anna knew Costa was considering possibilities, connecting the lines and drawing one right back to her. She was the only other person who had access to the information about Zoe Hunter and Costa's plans for her. Time for her to cut her losses, get out of the castle, and away from Costa. She was about to slip away from the door when she noticed the leather tube propped against the leg of the desk. It was here. Her time here wouldn't be a total loss, after all.

THE road to the castle twisted back on itself as it wound steeply up the forested hillside in a series of hairpin turns that became tighter as they neared the top. A few houses clustered at the base of the road near the town, but the rest of the road was deserted and unlit, a quiet passage between thick bands of evergreen.

The road was clear of snow, but a layer of it, about an inch deep, covered the trees and forest floor, brightening the night. There was enough moonlight that they could see the outlines of the road and the trees. They didn't speak as they hurried up the road, concentrating on keeping their footing. As they neared the top, a round tower in pale brown stone topped with a conical black roof came into view. Several windows in the tower glowed with light.

The road made one final curve back on itself before it reached the castle gates. They paused in the center of the road, the valley spread below them and the tower looming overhead.

The view was stunning. The lights of the village filled the hollow on the right side of the mountain, while on the left, a wall of rock plunged down to a wide gray lake that reflected the stars. Winded from the fast climb, Zoe's words came out in choppy white wisps of breath. "Are you sure you never saw Sam here or around Costa?"

She had spoken quietly, and Jack replied in the same low voice. "Yes. He hasn't been here. I'd remember him."

"But him being here...it can't be a coincidence."

Jack studied the wall extending out from the tower. "No, it can't."

"He's associated with Costa in some way," Zoe said, feeling as if she might be sick. "Everything about him—it was *all* a lie. I mean, I realized he'd been lying to me, but I thought some of it was true."

Jack took a set of keys out of his pocket. "Some of it probably was real. It wouldn't be the first time Costa set someone up in a business," Jack said grimly.

"But the things, he said to me, he acted like—" Zoe stopped abruptly, remembering the flirty innuendo, the intense gazes. And she'd fallen for it—all of it. She felt herself flushing as she remembered how flustered she'd been when he tried to kiss her at the airport. He'd probably been laughing inside the whole time.

"He probably meant every word of what he said to you—whatever it was." Jack's gaze was on the keys, flicking through them as he searched for one. "I don't see how he could help falling for you. I couldn't." He looked up and locked his gaze on hers. Zoe could tell from his face that he was almost as surprised as she was at what he'd said.

What Sam had said and done faded in importance, and she was suddenly very aware of how close they were to each other, their warm breath mingling in the cold air. She wanted to say something, but couldn't find any words. She smiled instead. Jack leaned toward her slightly, giving her time to pull away.

She didn't make a conscious decision to kiss him. One minute they were standing close to each other, and the next his lips were on hers, and it wasn't only her knees that went quivery. She wrapped her arms around him, her only clear thought was that it felt so right, so exactly right.

Jack pulled his lips away and rested his forehead against hers.

"I don't see any reason to stop," Zoe said.

"Other than the fact that it's ten degrees?"

"I don't feel cold."

Jack made a sound deep in his throat and stepped back. "As always, my timing is impeccable." He looked over his shoulder at the castle. "We've got to do this now. Before they realize we're here."

Zoe nodded. "Right." She noticed that his breathing was as choppy as hers.

"But we will finish this discussion later," Jack said.

"Oh, I'll hold you to that, don't worry."

Jack raised an eyebrow, and Zoe felt another little tremor inside. Sure, she'd flirted with Sam and there had been an initial attraction, but she and Jack had something different, something deeper and more intimate.

Jack turned to the castle, his tone business-like. "Okay, we'll follow this low stone wall to the gates. I have a key in case they're locked, but I doubt they will be since Sam just drove up here. We'll circle through the parking area to a back entrance. We'd better not talk anymore. Just in case."

"Okay. Let's go." They moved silently along the wall to the wrought-iron gates that were at least twelve feet tall and had an intricate crest in the middle. They were open wide enough for a car to drive through. Their footsteps sounded loud in the quiet of the forest as they made their way across the gravel parking lot. Jack pointed to the small blue car that Sam had driven. It was parked next to a black Mercedes. A dusting of snow covered a faded red Fiat in the far corner of the parking area—Jack's car, Zoe assumed.

They continued on to the castle wall, which soared twenty feet above them. They walked along it for about three to four hundred feet, and then they came to a point where the wall had collapsed, creating a pile of stone.

"Up and over," Jack said under his breath.

Zoe followed him, placing her feet where he'd placed his as they scrambled upward. Zoe was aware of the dark valley below them and had a sense of moving higher, but she kept her attention focused on the stone in front of her. They crested the pile of rubble and moved down the other side into the dark courtyard with only a few stones skittering down the pile to announce their arrival. They both paused to listen.

There was a faint rustle of movement from the woods, a creature moving through the undergrowth.

They moved to the portion of the wall that connected with the tower. Jack used a key to open a wooden door, then murmured, "Watch your head," and ducked through the pointed doorframe. Zoe glided in behind him, pressed the door closed, and then followed him down a set of stone stairs to an underground corridor. The hall was narrow and lit only with single bulbs spaced so far apart that she had to take a few paces in the dark between each pool of light. The floor and walls were made of stone and the whole place was as cold as it was outside.

Finally, Jack stopped at one of the doors. It swung open when he touched it. He cursed under his breath and moved inside. Zoe followed slowly, taking in the bare accommodations. A wooden chest, its drawers gaping open, stood next to a plain armoire. An iron bedframe with a thick down comforter filled the rest of the room. The comforter was wrinkled and bunched as if it had been shoved to the side. "Good thing you don't mind living simply. Not very posh," Zoe said.

Jack went straight to the open doors of the armoire. "Servant's quarters." He rummaged around in his clothes. "Despite the romantic image, castle life wasn't very comfortable, not for most people. At least I have a shared bath," he said, nodding to the door at the side of the room. He turned from the armoire, his gaze raking the rest of the room.

"Where did you put it?" Zoe asked. There weren't many hiding places. The walls were closely-fitted stone and the furnishings, despite being bare, looked solid. Jack didn't answer. He squatted down. The armoire sat on feet that raised it a few inches off the floor. He reached under the armoire and ran his hand along the inside edge of the trim. He removed his hand and showed Zoe a dusty strip of tape. "Gone."

Zoe bit her lip. "All this way...and it's gone?" She hiked the messenger bag higher on her shoulder. "That's not good."

"No, in more ways than one." Jack tossed the tape away as he stood. "It means someone searched my room. They're suspicious of me. We've need to leave."

"At least, we've still got Bent's laptop."

"Give me a minute to change into some warmer clothes, and we'll get out of here." Jack was already moving to fish a hiking boot from under the bed. He found its mate across the room. From the pile of crumpled clothes, Jack pulled out a pair of dark pants, a pale blue shirt, and a cream sweater. "See if you can find my coat, will you? It's black," he said as he disappeared through a small door into a bathroom.

Zoe didn't want to hang around any longer, but she couldn't blame him for changing from the thin pants and windbreaker into warmer clothes. She found the coat under the comforter and handed it to him when he emerged from the bathroom, pulling on the hiking boots. He didn't bother to tie them, just shrugged into the coat and headed for the door.

"I can't believe we came all this way, and it's gone," Zoe said as Jack opened the door.

Sam stood in the hall, a gun in his hand. "Not gone." He opened his free hand. An orange flash drive rested in his palm. "Just moved to a new location."

20

J ack tensed, but Sam trained the gun on Zoe's head. Jack raised his hands. "Good choice," Sam said. "Now, a few rules. No talking and no sudden moves. Got it?"

They both nodded, Jack a slow, deliberate drop of his chin. Zoe's head bobbed jerkily as blood zinged through her body. She wanted to sprint away into the pool of darkness beyond the next naked light bulb, but the hall was so narrow, she didn't have any doubt that Sam would hit her if he fired the gun. And his expression was so different, intense and focused. He looked as if he'd fire the gun without a second thought.

"Let's make sure you didn't bring anything dangerous with you," Sam said as he patted them down.

Jack sent Zoe a warning look that conveyed, *don't do anything stupid*, as clearly as if he'd spoken aloud.

She sent him a look back. *Of course I'm not going to do anything stupid. He's got a gun.*

Somehow Jack managed to send her a smile with only his

eyes. Yep, he'd gotten the message and, weirdly, she felt reassured. Jack wasn't going to pieces or panicking. She wouldn't either, she vowed.

But it was hard to stay calm and focused when Sam pressed the gun to the back of her head and marched them up a set of circular stairs to a more luxurious area of the castle with drafty hallways lined with tapestries and faded rugs. He guided them to a room with an ornate wooden desk positioned between a massive fireplace and narrow windows set in a stone wall that overlooked the steeply curving road that ran down into the valley. The room looked like something out of *Architectural Digest*, the medieval issue. A fire crackled in the grate, the other three walls of the room were paneled in a dark wood and ringed with bookcases.

Sam shoved Zoe's shoulder roughly, pushing her into a chair. "Hands." He pointed to the arm of the chair, keeping the gun on her. Another man with a neck so thick that he probably couldn't wear turtlenecks, slipped plastic zip ties around her wrists and tightened them.

"Very good," Sam said pleasantly.

The guy with the oversized neck used the zip ties to secure Jack's wrists and ankles to the chair beside Zoe. Then he wrapped a thick dishcloth across his mouth and tied it at the back of his head.

"So, you're a liar, a thief, and you hold people against their will?" Anger at his lies and at the casual way he ordered them around simmered through her. Zoe tugged on her wrists, but the plastic held firm.

"I am a much more interesting person than you thought, aren't I?" He grinned and said, "Now I will take care of your beautiful ankles."

He was *enjoying* this, she realized. He liked having her restrained to a chair. A chill ran through her and it had nothing to do with the temperature in the room. Jack made a low growling sound.

Sam waved the other guy to the door, indicating he could leave. As the door closed behind him, Sam tossed her messenger bag on the desk then put down the gun and secured her ankles to the legs of the wooden chair. "Boots," he said, clearly displeased that he couldn't get to her ankles. "Ah well...later. No gag for you." He stood. "It will get in my way."

He leaned over her, his mouth inches from her ear. Zoe squished back against the chair. "I've been looking forward to this. It will be..." he leaned even closer and she could smell meat and beer on his breath as he whispered, "delightful." Staying close to her face, he tilted his head to look at Jack as he spoke to him. "I think I will kill you last. That way, you may watch what I do to her."

Cold fear washed away the surge of anger she'd felt earlier, and she broke out in a clammy sweat. This did not seem like the guy who'd flirted with her, who seemed so soft-spoken, and almost gentle. How could she have been so wrong about him? Her stomach churned. How had she ever thought he was attractive?

The door opened and Costa came inside. Sam stepped back, picked up the gun, and moved to the fireplace. Zoe recognized Costa from the pictures she'd seen in the news articles. He looked slightly older, a little more worn. He had a few more wrinkles around his eyes and on his forehead, but his lean, trim build was the same. "So, this is perfect. You arrived at just the right time." He sounded as if he were welcoming guests to a party. He waved to Sam, indicating he should leave. Sam didn't look as though he wanted to go, but he did, handing the flash drive to Costa before he left.

Above the gag, Jack's gaze was locked on Costa. Jack didn't even look tense. He held his hands loosely and his face looked calm. Zoe felt beads of sweat soaking into her clothes at her back and her armpits. How did Jack manage to look so cool, even gagged and tied to a chair?

Costa went to the fireplace and tossed another log on the blaze. "It's a bit smoky in here," he said as he used a poker to position the new log. "Must apologize for that." He replaced the poker in the stand on the hearth and crossed the room to crack one of the tall windows open an inch. Zoe shot a look at Jack as Costa turned his back to open the window.

Jack shook his head, a warning, which Zoe interpreted to mean don't say anything, which was fine with her. She was still trying to take in what had happened. She definitely had a down-the-rabbit-hole kind of feeling. Costa's tone and manner were so easy and normal, conversational even, as if they had dropped by for a visit, but she and Jack were restrained with zip ties, and Jack had a gag in his mouth.

"These old homes, not everything is perfect." Costa brushed his hands together and then checked his watch. "Now, let's see what you brought." Costa perched on the edge of the desk, flipped open Zoe's messenger bag and spilled out the contents. He picked up Bent's laptop and opened it. A few clicks and his foot, which had been swinging languidly, stopped abruptly.

He stood and closed the laptop then clasped it to his chest. "Well, this is certainly interesting. It shows you already know about my venture capital plan." He picked up the flash drive. "I assume this is what drew you here?"

Jack's face didn't change.

Costa opened a drawer and removed a narrow leather satchel with a long strap, a man bag. When she and Jack were in Italy, she'd seen them a lot. Practically every guy had one. They put the strap over one shoulder and wore it across their chests, the bag on one hip, which left their hands free to drive their mopeds. The satchel was big enough that the laptop fit inside it. He added the flash drive to the man bag then put it on the desk chair. He removed a set of keys from the center drawer of the desk and set them beside the blotter.

He glanced at his watch again then moved to a grouping of two cracked leather chairs on either side of a small table set up with a chessboard. It looked as if a game was in progress. Pieces ranged across the black and white squares. Costa ran his hand down the side of the chessboard. "I suppose you think you are my opponent in this elaborate game." He waved at one of the chairs. "I admit that dealing with you has been much more interesting than I'd anticipated. However, you are not my opponent."

Costa picked up a knight from the game board. "You are merely a piece on the board." He ran his finger over the ridge of the horse's mane on the game piece as he crossed to the desk. "And, as exciting as the game has been, it is time for you to go back in the box." Costa placed the game piece in a marble box on the desk and snapped it shut.

He did not look at Jack again. He walked to the door and stepped into the hall. Zoe caught a glimpse of Sam, waiting there before the door closed again.

"He's talking about killing you," Zoe hissed. The doors

looked thick, but she wasn't about to take a chance that Costa could hear her, so she kept her voice low. "And me, too, probably because I doubt they're going to take you out and leave me around to talk about it." Jack sent her a look. "I know that look," Zoe said. "I know you're telling me to keep calm and think and not lose my head, but he's serious, Jack."

Jack tried to speak, but the gag garbled his words into an indistinguishable murmur. He bent at the waist.

Had he passed out? "Jack, what's wrong? Are you feeling okay?" He moved, twisting his neck around and mumbled some more.

"What? I don't get it? You look like I feel when I try to do yoga. What are you doing?"

Jack threw himself back against the chair, panting around his gag, and sent her a look of frustration.

"I'm sorry. You know I'm no good at charades."

Jack rolled his eyes. He used his hand to point at her wrist, then at his face. He gripped the arms of his chair then jerked himself up with all his strength. The chair hopped half an inch in her direction.

"I get it," she said. If he could get close enough, he could lean over and she could untie the gag. The arms of the chair were too short and his upper body was too long for him to bend over and untie the gag from the back of his head, but she could do it, if he could get close enough. Then, maybe they could shift over to the desk and find something to cut the plastic ties. She grabbed the arms of her chair and heaved.

Her chair didn't move. Its high back reached above her head and was decorated with thick grooves and pinnacles. The legs of the sturdy chair were embedded in the deep carpet. Jack managed to shift his chair another half an inch. Zoe blew out a breath and heaved. Her chair popped up a few centimeters, then settled into the deep indentions of the carpet. Zoe tried again, her hair flopping forward around her eyes.

The only sounds in the room were their ragged breathing and the popping of the fire. She felt her face flush with exertion. "This is an excellent workout," she gasped. "If we get out of here, I think I'll make an infomercial. Chair hopping cardio." She could see Jack out of the corner of her eye, his head bobbing up and down. His cheeks bulged a bit above the gag, and she knew she'd made him smile.

Suddenly, a section of the wood-paneled wall swung open and a woman with a curvy figure and dark hair in an asymmetrical cut came into the room.

Jack and Zoe, who had both been in mid-hop, went still.

The woman didn't make eye contact with them.

Zoe exchanged a quick look with Jack, and he shrugged one shoulder as if he wasn't sure what the woman was doing. She went to the desk and set down a long cardboard tube she carried. She quickly picked up a leather tube that had been propped against the leg of the desk and put it beside the cardboard one. With a few swift movements, she switched the contents of the tubes, moving a roll of glossy poster-size paper from the cardboard tube to the leather tube and a roll of soft almost fabric-like material from the leather tube to the cardboard container she'd arrived with. She replaced the leather tube, propping it against the leg of the desk exactly as it had been, then she picked up the cardboard tube.

"Wait, don't go," Zoe said. "Please help us." This had to be the secretary Jack mentioned. "You're Anna, aren't you?" Of course she was with Costa, but maybe Zoe could convince her to help them.

She didn't reply, but did pause. "Please, Anna. Costa is going to kill us. We need to get out of here."

Anna examined the man bag in the desk chair, tossing the flap back as she said, "Costa never kills anyone. He's told Sam to do that." She looked at the laptop, then extracted the flash drive. "He's told Sam to arrange things for you. Of course, Costa doesn't want to know the details. That way he has deniability."

Zoe blinked at her matter-of-fact tone then found her voice. "And you're okay with that? You're going to stand by and let two innocent people be killed?"

Anna slipped the flash drive into the pocket of her jeans. "I won't be here."

"You're still a party to this. You're an accessory." Zoe had no idea if that was true, but she had to do what she could. "Please, just hand me a pair of scissors. That's all I need."

Anna looked at Zoe for the first time, and Zoe's heart sank. Anna's gaze was cold and remote. There was no sympathy, no ambivalence at all. "If you're involved with Costa, you're far from innocent."

Zoe licked her lips. "Then I'll have to scream." She felt Jack tense beside her. Anna ignored her, grabbed the tube then turned her back, but not before Zoe had seen a flare of fear in her face. "And even if you leave before they get here," Zoe continued, "I'll tell them what you did—that you switched something in those tubes and took the flash drive. I doubt you'd make it to the village before they catch up with you."

Anna stopped, her free hand flexing into a fist. Zoe

waited, her heart hammering as she watched Anna's hand open and close. Had she made things worse? Anna whirled toward Zoe, her chin lowered with a look on her face that made Zoe wish she'd kept quiet.

"And how do I know that you won't betray me, if I help you?"

Zoe sucked in a breath and hoped that Anna couldn't actually see her heartbeat through the fabric of her coat. "You don't. You'll have to trust us. Just as we'll have to trust you."

Anna studied her a moment, then strode toward the desk. She ripped open a drawer and pulled out a pair of scissors. She slammed them down on the edge of the desk near Zoe, and Zoe couldn't help flinching.

Anna kept her hand on top of the scissors. "We have a deal? We both keep quiet." Her gaze flicked between Zoe and Jack.

"Yes. We won't say anything," Zoe said as Jack nodded his head.

Anna removed her hand from the scissors. "Then you better move quickly. I overheard Costa. He told Sam to make your deaths look like an accident—no guns or anything that would draw extra police attention." She whipped around, strode to the door in the paneling.

The door slid into place. Jack and Zoe looked at each other for a moment, then both of them resumed their frantic chair hopping movements. Two heaves brought Zoe to the edge of the desk. She strained her fingers straight up and curled them over the tip of the scissors, then worked them around in her hand so that her fingers were through the grips. Zoe looked at Jack through the screen of hair that had fallen over her face.

He nodded at her. "Yes, I know it's only a few more times," Zoe said, "but I feel like I've climbed the highest wall at the gym." She blew out a breath and shook her hair back from her face. "Okay. Now we just have to rotate so that we're facing each other." Jack nodded and set to work shifting his chair into alignment with hers.

Zoe wrapped her fingers over the scissors as she grasped the chair arms. Two heaves brought her so close to Jack that the tip of the scissors nearly stabbed him as her chair came down. The metal point gouged the wood near his wrist as Jack jerked his hand away as far as the plastic ties allowed.

"Well, that should do it," Zoe said between breaths. She worked the scissors into the groove of space between Jack's wrist and the plastic and sawed away with the scissors. The plastic was thick, and it took her several strokes with the scissors for the metal to bite into the plastic. Then the scissors snapped closed, and the plastic tie fell to the carpet.

A creaking sound came from the hallway.

Zoe's head snapped up. "He's back."

Jack grabbed the arms of the chair and began shifting it back into the position it had been when Costa left the room. Zoe managed to bring her chair around so that it was facing the desk, but she was far closer to the desk than she had been, but it was too late. She couldn't move anymore because the door swung open. Costa entered.

Zoe pushed the handle of the scissors up under her wrist and tried to calm her breathing, not that it would do much good if he looked directly at her. She was sure the flush on her translucent skin matched her hair, which was probably twice its normal size.

But Costa didn't even look at them. As he crossed the

room to a tall bookcase, he checked his watch then he moved several books to the side, revealing a safe. He punched in a code, opened the door, and removed an envelope. He closed the safe, replaced the books, then returned to the desk where he put the envelope in the bottom left drawer of the desk.

Zoe had her breathing under control and was trying to figure out what to say—if there was anything to say—that would convince him to let them go, but before she could decide on an approach, Costa slung the man bag over one shoulder, grabbed the leather tube, and picked up the set of keys from the desktop.

He paused, fingered the Mercedes logo on the remote key fob, then seemed to come to a decision and replaced it on the desk. He left the room without once looking at them.

He left the door to the hallway open, so Zoe whispered, "He's leaving, isn't he?"

Jack nodded.

"He doesn't want to be here when..." Zoe trailed off, and Jack gripped the arms of the chair.

"Right. Back at it," Zoe said, but before she could gather her strength to move the chair, Sam entered the room with his attention focused squarely on them. Jack kept his free arm positioned exactly as it would have been if the tie still held it in place. He wanted the element of surprise, she realized. It was all they had left, she supposed, except for the scissors. If only she had handed them to Jack, he would have had a weapon. He was the one who'd taken years of martial arts. She'd only had a few piddly lessons. If one of them was going to take on Sam, she wanted it to be Jack.

The metal handles of the scissors felt cold on the inside of her wrist. She didn't think she could be very effective with them unless Sam got really close to her, and if he did...could she stab him? Would she be able to do that?

Sam paced over to them. He held the gun loosely in his right hand. It dangled beside his leg as he studied them. "Been working hard, I see. You've discovered those chairs are good, sturdy German craftsmanship."

Zoe managed to sneak a look at Jack's wrist and saw the cuff of his sleeve covered the missing plastic tie, but the tie itself lay on the carpet under the chair. Zoe hoped the intricate pattern of the carpet would hide it.

She looked up from the carpet. "Everything is in place, ready to go. You are going to have a very bad car accident," Sam said with mock sadness. Then his voice changed. "But I do believe we have time for a little fun before you have to go." He fixed his gaze on Zoe. "You have no idea how long I've looked forward to this," he said, his voice going thick.

Yes, I think I can stab him, no problem, Zoe decided. She licked her lips. "Sam, you don't want to be part of this. Costa can't run from the police forever. He will get caught, and you'll go down with him."

Out of the corner of her eye, Zoe saw Jack's fist clench.

Sam didn't reply. It was as if he hadn't heard a word she'd said. He came around the desk on Zoe's side. He propped himself up, legs splayed on either side of her chair, and reached out.

"You don't want to do this," Zoe said again.

"Yes, I do." He ran a finger along her cheek, then trailed his fingertips down her neck to the base of her throat where her pulse fluttered. Zoe gave up on talking and concentrated on not gagging. He wasn't listening; it wouldn't do any good to try to talk her way out of this situation.

His attention focused only on Zoe. "You had no idea, did you? I had you so convinced I was a sensitive, caring, metrosexual type that if I'd told you the things I've done, you never would have believed me."

He leaned close to her face. "Would you have believed I had it in me to kill a man?"

Zoe had a feeling that this was one of those trick questions that she'd answer wrong, no matter what she said, so she kept quiet.

He exhaled and leaned back. "Killing is easy, simple even, if you do it with a gun or a knife." He lifted the gun as he spoke and pointed it at her chest. Zoe's breath caught, and she tried not to move an inch.

He dropped his arm to his side. "It's killing without leaving a trace that's difficult. Like what I did to Bent. They'll never know he was dead before the fire began."

"You did that to him?" Zoe couldn't help asking. "You poisoned him?"

"Noticed that, did you? Well, there won't be any evidence of it for the police to find. The fire erased any trace of the poison or my presence there." With one hand, Sam reached out and popped open the top button of her coat.

She scrunched back in the chair as far as she could. Sam laughed. "Oh, don't go all timid on me." She worked the handle of the scissors into the palm of her hand. He was so focused on her face and neck that he didn't even notice. If he'd just come a little closer she could shove the metal point into his leg.

The sound of a car engine carried through the slightly open window. The engine struggled, then died. Sam's attention strayed from the second button of Zoe's coat as he tilted his head toward the window. There was a beat of silence, then the engine labored again and caught. It sputtered as if were about to die again, but the driver revved the engine, and it settled into a bumpy rhythm. Zoe's grip tightened on the scissors.

Sam turned away, caught sight of the keys on the desktop and snatched them up, his face confused. He sprinted to the window, pushed it wide. "Not that car! No!"

21

Sam dropped the keys, leaned over the ledge of stone that protruded out from the window, and waved his left arm as he shouted. He still held the gun in his right hand down by his leg.

Jack reached across Zoe and took the scissors in his free hand. He quickly cut the ties on his other arm, his ankles, and cut Zoe's hands and ankles free as well. Sam, his back turned to them, waved and shouted, but the engine continued to run. A yellow glow brightened the windows. The driver had turned the headlights on, but the engine continued to idle.

Jack shoved the scissors in his back pocket, handles down, then untied the knot holding the gag in place. He yanked it off as he moved to the fireplace and took the poker from the hearth, the carpet masking the sounds of his movements. By the time Zoe stood up, Jack had crossed the room to Sam.

Sam turned slightly, caught sight of Jack, and raised his arm with the gun. Jack froze as Sam leveled the gun at him.

Frantically, Zoe looked around. What could she do? The chair was too heavy for her to do more than shove it a few feet. She'd never be able to throw it through the air and hit Sam. He was too far away. Jack had the scissors. The desk had nothing on it except a few pens, the blotter, and the marble box with the chess piece.

The car engine continued to idle. The corners of Sam's mouth turned up. Zoe snatched the pens and threw them, reached for the blotter and tossed it. The cascade of office supplies didn't deter Sam, he only raised his shoulder to block the pens from hitting him in the face.

Her hand closed on the marble box. She heaved it across the room. This time, Sam raised his arm and ducked his head. The box sailed over his head and crashed into the stone window ledge. Jack lunged forward and brought the poker down on the back of Sam's head. He dropped to the floor.

"Is he...?" Zoe asked as she tried to catch her breath.

Jack picked up the gun then pushed on Sam's shoulder with his foot, rolling him onto his back. Jack cautiously placed two fingers at Sam's throat then looked up. "He's alive," he said, his voice scratchy.

"That's...good. I guess."

Jack ran a hand down over his mouth and cleared his throat. "As long as we get out of here before he wakes up."

The things from the desktop that Zoe had tossed at Sam were scattered around him. One of them, an index card, caught her eye because of the neatly printed word, Evergreen. She picked up the card. "Hey, look at this. It must have been under the blotter on the desk—"

She stopped speaking because the noise of the car engine, which had been filtering into the room, changed tone. A flash of headlights cut through the black square of the window. Jack stepped over Sam, and Zoe joined him at the window. It was the little blue car that Sam had driven up the road. "Do you think Costa's in that?" Zoe pushed the index card into her pocket as she looked to the parking area where a sleek black Mercedes rested beside the red Fiat.

"Sam thought he was."

As the car neared the gates, the red brake lights flared, but the car didn't slow. It continued to roll. The car swung onto the road that curved to the right and ran alongside the castle wall, dropping steeply to the first hairpin turn on the side of the mountain with the village below it.

The brake lights continued to glow red, but instead of slowing, the car picked up speed. It swung wide into the turn. One wheel slipped off the surface of the road and bumped along the dirt and leaves. The driver corrected and the car was back on the asphalt surface, picking up even more speed as it barreled toward the next hairpin turn.

The car careened down the steep descent, racing toward the drop off and the icy lake below. It reached the turn and sailed straight into the air, disappearing over the precipice into the sky, brake lights shining red. Zoe felt her heartbeat thud twice in the silence then there was a distant splash.

Zoe realized she'd reached for Jack's hand. "That was supposed to be us."

Jack nodded and glanced at Sam.

"What about him?" Zoe asked.

"Leave him." The words came out rough, and Jack cleared his throat. He used the edge of his coat to wipe the gun clean, then dropped it beside Sam. "We'll be gone before he' awake." He plucked the Mercedes keys from the carpet.

Zoe took one more look at Sam then hurried to catch up with Jack, who was already across the room, pushing the door open. Zoe thudded into Jack's back when he stopped abruptly.

"Wh—? Jack threw his hand up and his shoulders were so tense that Zoe instantly went quiet. She heard the sound of footsteps in the hall, then a door nearby—in the next room? —opened and closed.

Jack grabbed her hand, and they moved to the door in the paneling where Anna had entered the room. "There's a man checking every room. He just looked in here," he said as they slipped through the door in the paneling. The next room was another office, set up with a desktop computer, filing cabinets, and a copier.

Before Jack could close the door in the paneling completely, a man entered the office where Sam was still sprawled on the floor. Jack held the door open a few centimeters. Zoe ducked under his arm, so she could see, too.

He was a short man; the black overcoat he wore flapped around his ankles a few inches above the ground. His gelled black hair was combed straight back from his fleshy face, which was covered in shallow pockmarks, probably scars from bouts with severe acne. He studied Sam then closed the window with a solid click.

Zoe looked up at Jack with her eyebrows raised.

Jack shrugged and mouthed, "Don't know who he is."

The man stood over Sam for a moment then reached inside his coat, pulled out a gun, and shot Sam in the chest.

Zoe sucked in her breath then clamped a hand over her mouth. They must have been too far way for the man to hear r, because he didn't look their way. After checking for a pulse, he put the gun in his coat pocket and pulled on a set of gloves.

He moved around the desk, opened a bottom drawer on the left, and removed the envelope Costa had placed there. He lifted the flap and flicked his fingers along a thick stack of paper. Even from across the room, Zoe could see the blue color and the flash of a silver stripe. They were euros, a huge stack of twenties. The man replaced the money in the envelope then tucked it away in an interior pocket of his coat. He shoved the drawer closed with his knee then removed the gloves, stuffing them in his pocket.

Footsteps pounded along the hallway. The man removed the gun from his pocket and went around the desk, knelt beside Sam, and reached out as if he were checking for a pulse.

The door opened and several men in police uniforms moved cautiously inside, their guns raised. Zoe expected them to arrest the man in the overcoat, but they relaxed and holstered their weapons when the man in the overcoat spoke to them in German.

"What is going on?" Zoe mouthed.

Jack put his lips to her ear. "The guy says he's with the federal German police force, I think. The other men in uniform are local. The Federal guy says he came to arrest Sam Clark because he's wanted in connection with an arson and murder in England. He says Sam charged at him, and he had no choice but to shoot him." The man produced papers as he spoke, which seemed to satisfy the uniformed men. One of them nodded and gestured to the hallway.

Jack eased the door closed, but still whispered. "They're fanning out to search the building. They're looking for a woman with black hair in her late twenties who is also wanted by the Federal German police."

"I don't want to stick around and try to explain why we're here, especially after watching that guy shoot Sam."

Jack nodded in agreement, still trying to listen through the door.

"I suppose the hallway is out?" Zoe said.

"Unfortunately, yes. And there's no convenient secret passage way either."

"Then that means we either hide or go out a window," Zoe said, looking doubtfully at the windows, which were the same as the ones in the other office, set deep into the thick stone.

"We're not both fitting under the desk. It's got to be the window," Jack said, grimly. "No other choice."

They crossed the room, and Zoe crawled onto the ledge then pushed one of the windows open.

"Okay, it's not too bad." Zoe stepped through the narrow opening and found a foothold. "It's not a straight vertical drop. Only about a foot down and then the wall flares out."

"That's called the talus." Jack twisted his shoulders sideways and maneuvered through the window. "Made it harder for enemies to scale the wall and build siege works, not to mention the thicker walls were harder to break through."

"Well, you're a font of interesting information."

"I had quite a bit of time to read all the brochures on the castle."

Zoe threw her head back to check his progress. He was still perched by the window, hanging onto the stone ledge. "Come on, you're delaying. There's toe holds and everything. The mortar or grout or whatever you call it has worn away between the stones, and you can climb down it just like a ladder."

"You're not making me feel better about this," Jack said, but dropped his leg down and wiggled his foot around until he had it wedged into an opening.

"Now, your other foot," Zoe coached, shifting to the left so she could see him better. He moved lower, and his booted foot came down level with her head, the untied shoelaces dangling on either side of the shoe.

Zoe decided it would be better not to mention the untied shoelaces. Instead she said, "You're doing great. Move your hands down now. We're on the flared part, so it'll be easy now."

"Speak for yourself," Jack muttered.

"So don't think about the climb. Tell me what you think happened up there. You saw the money? It can only mean one thing, right?"

"Costa set up Sam and Anna," Jack confirmed.

Zoe continued to move her feet and hands at Jack's slower pace.

"Do you think they'll find Anna? Could she still be in the castle?" Zoe paused to look at the parking lot below them. "The cars are still there—except for the blue one," Zoe said and felt a little sick, remembering the flare of useless brake lights against the night sky.

"She's probably already on a train. It doesn't take long to walk down to the village. There's a trail I've used many times. Only takes about fifteen minutes. She probably left before Costa. She seemed like the type who could figure out when she should disappear."

"She was intent on getting out of there," Zoe said as she

checked their progress. "Just a little farther." To keep him talking she said, "Even if Costa paid off the guy in the overcoat, won't it be obvious that he shot Sam while Sam was on his back?"

"Somehow I don't think the investigation will be very thorough. I bet the overcoat guy will make sure there's only a cursory inquiry. Of course, Sam was supposed to finish us off before the overcoat man arrived."

"Costa did check his watch several times while he was with us like he had an appointment to keep."

"Or like he wanted to be gone before the overcoat guy showed up."

"We're down." Zoe's feet touched the ground of the parking lot, which was more crowded than when they arrived with two police cars and another brown car with no official markings on it.

Jack dropped down beside her and dusted his hands off. "We really must stop making a habit of this," he said as he pulled the Mercedes key fob out of his pocket and pressed a button. There was a corresponding click from the sleek black car parked near the gates as the doors unlocked.

"We're taking Costa's car?" Zoe asked uneasily.

"Unless you want to walk back down?"

Zoe moved to the passenger door. "Not really, but what if there are more police on the road? What if they recognize the car?"

"That's what I'm counting on."

Their doors closed with a solid, expensive sound. Jack started the engine and drove forward a few feet, then stopped abruptly a few times. Zoe clutched the dashboard.

"Just checking the brakes," he said easily. "I didn't think

Sam would have messed with this car, but I wanted to make sure." Jack hit the headlights as he pulled through the gates and drove to the hairpin turn where the blue car had gone over the edge. He put the car in park, and they got out. Zoe edged up to the side of the road.

Jack looked over his shoulder at her. "Don't tell me you're nervous, standing here. You're not the one who is afraid of heights."

"It's the fall that I'm worried about," she quipped, and he smiled at her. She looked at the drop, and her smile faded. "And a fall off this..." she shivered. The rock dropped in a sheer face down to the flat plane of the water.

"Would be fatal," Jack finished for her. "Look," Jack said, pointing to a smattering of lights about a quarter of a mile farther along the edge of the water where there was a strip of flat ground.

"Are those headlights?" Zoe asked.

"I think so. Probably heard the crash and went to investigate. They won't be able to do anything except pull the car off the bottom." Jack turned to the Mercedes. "Time to go." This time, Jack took the sweeping hairpin curves in a carefree manner, his hands loose on the steering wheel. The car slalomed to the base of the mountain, and Zoe reminded herself that she liked exciting rides. Of course, this descent was very different from her favorite rollercoaster rides.

As they approached the village, Zoe saw a lone police car slanted halfway across the narrow road. "It's a road block." An officer stepped from the car as they approached.

Jack slowed the car, rolled closer. Zoe braced herself, sure that Jack was about to floor it and make the officer jump out of the way, but the man stepped aside and waved them forward.

"Not for this car, it isn't." Jack said. "He thinks we're Costa. Put your scarf over your hair and look away," Jack said as they neared the officer. Zoe fumbled with her scarf and managed to cover most of her hair then looked down at the stitching on the leather seats. The car came even with the officer, and Jack raised his hand in a wave that also managed to block his face. Jack nosed the car through the small gap between the grill of the police car and the stucco wall of a building, then accelerated into the town square. "And, we're out of here," Jack said following the sign that pointed them in the direction of the Autobahn.

THREE hours later, Zoe sat at a small table in a travel plaza off the busy road, her hands wrapped around a cup of coffee as she surveyed the parking lot where they'd left the Mercedes.

Jack, seated across from her, noticed her gaze. "They're not coming after us."

"I still can't believe we weren't stopped." They had spent the drive in silence, both of them tense and watching the mirrors, waiting for flashing lights to appear.

"I was pretty sure Costa had paid off the local cops, too. He was able to move around so freely," Jack said, then sipped his coffee. "Hey." He tapped her hand, drawing her attention away from the window. "I wouldn't have stopped if it wasn't safe."

Zoe stared at Jack. "No, you wouldn't," she said slowly. That was the thing with Jack. She knew, deep down—even if she didn't want to admit it to herself—she knew in her core that Jack was trying to keep her safe. The same certainly couldn't be said for Sam.

"What's wrong?" Jack set his cup down. "You feeling okay?"

"Just having to deal with some monumental lapses in judgment. I can't believe Sam deceived me. And, I'm having a hard time wrapping my head around the fact that he's dead." Zoe leaned forward and whispered, "*Dead*. That man just shot him, didn't even flinch. I know Sam did some terrible things—"

"Like killing Bent and setting his office on fire, not to mention he was going to kill us, too. There's no halfway with these people. They're all-in and they'll do whatever it takes to protect themselves. That's why I didn't contact you directly during the summer."

Zoe nodded. "I understand that now." She traced the rim of her cup with her finger. "That car crash...do you think they'll find him?"

"Costa?" Jack asked. "I'm sure they'll dredge the lake and pull out the car. There's no way he survived the impact." They sat in silence for a few moments then Jack said, "The laptop is gone, too. Even if they find it, the chances of it being intact and anyone being able to recover information from it...less than zero. And that's not even considering the fact that if it were found, we'd have to convince someone to try and recover the data."

"Too bad we can't just access the draft emails," Zoe said. "They're out there in cyberspace."

"Somewhere," Jack said. "But we don't know where to look." Jack pushed his empty cup away and shook his head.

"No, Bent was too smart to write down his password info and even if he did, his office burned."

"But won't the police realize Bent, Sam, and Costa are linked and investigate? Track down his emails?"

"I don't think the police will be anxious to broadcast that they were using a 'cyber crime expert' who was also perpetrating cyber crime himself. And if the overcoat guy is any indication of the type of investigators on the case...well, let's just say I'm not holding out hope that they'll find anything."

Zoe sipped her coffee, then sat up straight. "What about Costa, then?"

"What?"

"Well, maybe Bent was too savvy to write down his passwords, but Costa wasn't a computer geek." Zoe plunged her hands into her pockets and felt the stiff paper. She pulled it out, a smile breaking across her face. "Maybe Costa was just like the majority of people, who write down their passwords and keep them close to their computer."

"What is that?" Jack asked in a cautious voice.

"I found it on the floor after you took out Sam. I think it was on the desk, under the blotter, and I tossed it when I was throwing everything I could find. I noticed it, but then we heard the blue car, and I stuffed it into my pocket and forgot all about it until now. Look at these," she said, her voice bubbling with excitement as she scanned the short list of numbers and letters. "This line, vc2db@mail.com. That's their initials. Victor Costa to Dave Bent. That's probably the user ID and the word beside it, Evergreen, is probably the password." Zoe sat back, relieved. "We didn't lose the draft emails after all."

Jack rubbed his hand over her jaw as he looked at the card. "I think you're right."

"Then why don't you look happier?"

"Because I need to tell you something, and I know you're not going to like it."

"You're scaring me."

"It's nothing bad. At least, once you get over one minor point, it won't be. Besides, you like surprises."

"I do," Zoe said, cautiously.

He picked up a plastic knife from the table, propped one foot on top of his knee and then applied the blade of the knife to the grooves on the sole of the hiking boot. He wiggled the knife around, and a section of the sole popped out. He pulled out a small, oblong bundle of plastic that was wedged into the hole. He handed the piece of plastic to her. "I know how you feel about secrets, but this couldn't be helped. Too much commotion to tell you about it at the time. And, I want it on the record that I told you about it as soon as it was safe."

She unwrapped the plastic. "This is a flash drive." Zoe's eyebrows were drawn down in a frown. "It's not *the* flash drive....is it?"

He nodded.

"But the other one...the orange one?"

"Decoy. I thought it would be good to have two. This one is the real one, the one with the evidence about Costa."

"And the other one? What's on it?"

"Gibberish. Coded, of course, so that it would take them a while to figure it out. And a few pictures of cats for good measure."

"Do you know what this means?" Zoe fell back against

her chair. "It means we can prove neither you nor I were involved in the scam or hiding the money. We're in the clear."

"In the clear," he said, slowly as if testing the words out.

"Yeah." Zoe nodded. "You know what else it means?" Zoe didn't wait for an answer. "It means I can teach you to climb properly."

He waved his hand. "Oh, no. I've had enough climbing to last me a lifetime, thank you very much."

"Come on. It'll be easy. This time you'll have a harness."

SUNRISE lit the white-tipped mountaintops that surrounded Geneva as Jack and Zoe entered the airport.

"You didn't have to walk me in," Zoe said.

"Yes, I did."

"Mort will meet me when the plane lands in Newark, and I'll hand the flash drive over to him. It will all be fine. I know you feel skittish about coming back, but I don't see why you won't come with me now instead of waiting."

"Because I don't have quite the same faith in the FBI that you do. I rather like the idea of making sure there are no handcuffs in my future before I get on an airplane."

"Fine," Zoe said. They'd already gone around and around on the topic during the drive to the airport, and Zoe could tell she wasn't going to change his mind. "Where will you go while you wait?"

"I'm not telling you anything. I'll stay out of sight until I hear from you," he said, raising a hand that held a cheap cell phone. Zoe patted her pocket, which contained the twin to his phone.

They'd done a bit of shopping with their dwindling supply of cash before they reached the airport. First, they'd found an Internet café and emailed a copy of the draft emails to Mort, then Zoe had broken out her last credit card that wasn't maxed out, and paid the change fee so that she could fly from Geneva to Dallas. There was no point in staying off the grid once she'd sent the email to Mort.

"You better not lose that phone," Zoe said.

"Wouldn't dream of it."

"I mean it. If you disappear, I'll find you. I've done it twice now. I can do it again."

The skin around Jack's eyes crinkled as he smiled. "I don't doubt it for a minute."

"I'm serious."

"So am I."

"Good." Zoe blew out a breath and checked the monitors. She needed to get going. "Right. Okay. Well, this is it."

Jack's arm encircled her. "No, this isn't it." He kissed her quickly on the lips. "Once all this mess around Costa gets cleared up, there's a few things we need to sort out. Things just between you and me," he said then pulled away.

She gripped his coat and drew him back to her. "Is that a promise or a challenge?" she whispered, teasing his lips with hers.

"Consider it a bit of both." He managed to get the words out before his lips came down on hers.

EPILOGUE

One week later

Sato placed an envelope on the corner of Mort's desk.

"What's this?" Mort asked, eyeing it over the frame of his half glasses.

Sato propped himself up on a nearby desk and sipped from his tall Starbucks to-go cup. "Retirement present."

Mort frowned then opened the envelope gingerly. He pulled out a license plate frame and snorted as he read the lettering around the edge: "I'm retired. Go around me."

"Not nearly as bad as I thought it might be," Mort said. "Thanks."

Sato raised his cup in acknowledgement. "Don't worry, that's just the first of many. Your party is next week. I'm sure the presents will get worse." He looked toward the open file on Mort's desk. "Jack Andrews case?" At Mort's nod, Sato asked, "Will it be wrapped up before you leave?"

"Almost. Once he finishes answering the Brit's questions, Andrews will be able to come back. No charges pending."

"So the ex-wife's story checked out?"

Mort took off his glasses and rolled his chair away from his desk an inch. "Amazingly, yes."

"The emails in the draft folder were legit?"

Mort nodded. "Yep. Costa planned the whole shebang from the get-go. Hooked Jack Andrews and drew him in, then set him up to be the patsy."

Sato made a clicking sound. "Slick. And the money?"

"The tech guys are sorting through Costa's accounts. He had Bent juggling his money through multiple accounts around the world. It will take a while, but they'll find it."

"Probably not before you go."

"Doubtful. But everything else checks out. Several of Zoe Hunter's neighbors remember a white van parked on the street for several days. One person even called in and reported it as suspicious, so we have a plate. It's registered to Wade Selinger of Muskogee, Illinois, who has apparently skipped town. Moved out of his apartment during the night. We ran down his family in Cleveland, but they haven't heard from him. I'm sure we'll get him someday."

Mort closed the file and tossed his glasses on top of it. "Her car did have a tracker on it, and once the computer guys actually get their hands on her computer from the British, it will probably have one as well. Find anything on Sam Clark?"

Sato reached over to his desk and pulled out a sheet of paper. "Small time musician from Bakersfield. He did have a store that sold used musical instruments, which was suspected of being involved in money laundering for Costa. The cops over there were never able to charge him. From what we can piece together with the phone records and the emails between Costa and Sam Clark, Costa offered to underwrite him, set him up in business in Dallas with the understanding that he'd stay close to Zoe Hunter and keep an eye out in case Jack showed up."

Sato handed the sheet of paper to Mort, who took it, but pointed back at Sato with it, "You called that one, that he wasn't dead."

Sato shook his head. "Just a feeling."

"You got a feeling about this Anna Whitmore? Where she might be?"

Sato shook his head. "Nothing yet."

"Guess I have to leave that part with you. Let me know what happens."

"Sure. I'll come play checkers with you and give you an update. I figure you'll be going crazy in two weeks."

"You'll have a long trip. In two weeks, I'll be in the middle of the Caribbean. Kathy's booked us on a cruise."

"You almost sound like you're looking forward to it."

"This retirement idea sounds better and better every day."

ANNA studied the mountain valley from the window, squinting against the glare of the sunlight on the snow. The tube with the painting jostled against her leg with the movement of the train. Now that she was sure she'd gotten away clean, her next step was to find a place to store the painting. Then she could seek out buyers, but there was no rush. She had all the time in the world. No one would ever come after her.

She opened the letter from Costa's printer, read over it again. The instructions were detailed and convoluted, as all of Costa's plans were, but it all boiled down to a simple result. Costa instructed Bent to move the GRS money to a new account, using a digital trail that could be followed. He was to cover his tracks, of course—he couldn't make it too easy—but he wasn't to cover them too well. Costa wanted the digital money trail to be discovered.

She smiled at the thought of some analyst in a dreary cubical in the States following the money from one bank account to another, finally running it down to a single, empty account with the name Zoe Hunter on it. How nice that the account would show Zoe had used the money to purchase an expensive painting from a shady Paris art dealer.

Anna refolded the letter and relaxed into her seat, debating where she'd settle down. The south of France was nice...but she'd always wanted to see Capri.

THE END

Get exclusive excerpts of upcoming books and member-only giveaways: Sara's Notes and News at SaraRosett.com/signup.

THE STORY BEHIND THE STORY

Thanks for reading *Secretive*! This is my second outing with Zoe and Jack, and this adventure was as much fun to write as their first one. I hope you enjoyed it. If you'd take a moment to rate or review *Secretive* online, I'd appreciate it.

You can check out pictures that inspired me as well as photos from my trip to Germany at the *Secretive* board on Pinterest. You can find out more about me and my books at my website, SaraRosett.com, or you can sign up for my non-annoying updates. I hope you'll connect with me on Facebook, Twitter, Pinterest, or Goodreads. Happy reading!

ALSO BY SARA ROSETT

This is Sara's complete catalogue at the time of publication, but new books are in the works. To be the first to find out when Sara has a new book, sign up for her updates.

On the Run series

Elusive

Secretive

Deceptive

Suspicious

Devious

Treacherous

Murder on Location series

Death in the English Countryside

Death in an English Cottage

Death in a Stately Home

Death in an Elegant City

Menace at the Christmas Market (novella)

Death in an English Garden

Death at an English Wedding

CPSIA information can be obtained
at www.ICGtesting.com
Printed in the USA
LVHW092128300921
699190LV00015B/116

9 780998 253565